Cupcake

The Fluffy Cupcake Book 1

Katie Mettner

Katie Mettner

Cupcake

For the real Hay-Hay.
Thanks for being the best taste-tester in the county.

Katie Mettner

One

Ask anyone in Lake Pendle, Minnesota, where to find the best baked goods in a fifty-mile radius, and they'll point you to me, Haylee Davis, co-owner of The Fluffy Cupcake. Admit it. The name is delightful. If it doesn't conjure up the image of a perfectly capped sponge cake with buttercream icing covered in a smattering of sprinkles, or, if you're lucky, one of my homemade chocolates sitting atop that puff of goodness, there's something wrong with you. My bakery is everyone's favorite place to be from the moment the first whiff of fresh bread wafts into the air until the last cupcake leaves the case. Every special occasion, birthday, wedding, and funeral starts with a pickup or delivery from The Fluffy Cupcake.

Lake Pendle is a Hallmark movie set waiting to happen. We still have an old-fashioned Main Street, and it's packed with traditional businesses to keep our residents stocked with what they need year-round. Big box stores haven't invaded the beauty of our little town yet, and that is just one of the reasons tourists come back every summer to spend time on the beautiful blue waters.

"Here you are, Mrs. McCracken. Have a good day and thanks for stopping at The Fluffy Cupcake."

"Thank you, Haylee. You've made my day. You know how much I love your Top O' the Morning muffins!"

I waved as the gray-haired lady of nearly nine decades accepted her box of muffins and toddled on down the sidewalk.

"Quick, lock the door!" Amber, my best friend and business partner, yelled from behind me.

I hurried to the door, laughing the whole way, and flipped over the sign from open to closed. Once locked, I leaned against the door to take a deep breath.

"What a day," I moaned before walking back behind the bakery counter. "We sold out of everything, and I lost track of how many special orders we took in. I'm going to be here for hours this weekend just trying to catch up."

"And you love every minute of it," came a voice from the kitchen.

The man behind the voice strode toward us in all of his handsome glory. The thought alone had me forcing myself not to roll my eyes. Brady Pearson wore an apron, a hairnet, and a grin that went on for miles. Cocky, self-absorbed, and incorrigible were the only three words you needed to describe the man. Sure, some women liked to add handsome, muscular, and good enough to eat, but I wasn't one of them. Okay, so I was, but what I wasn't was stupid enough to admit it to him. He didn't need the encouragement. Guys like Brady had one thing on their mind—sex. Not the monogamous kind, either. They lived for sex, and lots of it, with a different woman every night. I wasn't judging, to each their own, but I wasn't going to be one of those women, no matter how many times he implied that he'd like me to be.

"You look tired, cupcake," he said, his voice oozing soothing charm. It made my blood boil.

I took a step forward and dug my finger into his hard, highly muscled chest. "Do not call me cupcake, cupcake." I ran my finger up his chest until it smacked him under the chin with purpose.

He grasped my shoulders and shook them, his silky dishwater blond hair shifting around under his chef's cap from the movement. "You need to loosen up. You're not even thirty, but you act like a grandma ready for the nursing home."

This time, my brow went down slowly while his went up. He loved to goad me into a heated argument about who was more immature, him, or a six-month-old kitten. He usually won the contest every time. "Why aren't you working? I would like to go home at some point today. I can't do that until you've handed over your inventory form and prepared the cooler for delivery."

"You got big plans tonight, Chef Davis?" Brady's lips turned up in a smile, and the sun from the front window glinted off his perfectly straight white teeth, nearly blinding me.

I held my arms out wide. "Huge ones, they include stuffing a sock this long in your mouth!"

Amber laughed melodically next to me and stuck an arm in to separate us. "Children, children," she tisked. "If you can't get along, I'll have to get out the sharing shirt. Then you'll have to touch each other."

The mutual eye roll she got did nothing but make her laugh. "I'm not sharing anything with him," I muttered before I turned my back to him and started counting the money in the till.

Brady chuckled, and I hated that I had to bite back a smile at the sound. He did have the best laugh I'd ever heard. "You know I love you, Chef Cupcake," he said, kissing my cheek.

"Awww, and what would I do without you, cookie britches?" I asked sweetly, batting my lashes at him over my shoulder.

"Gag me with a cupcake," came Amber's dramatic response.

We all laughed at the same time and I hip-checked Brady on my way by to my office where the safe was. "Seriously, though, Brady. I need the inventory done, and the cooler prepped."

Brady flipped his towel down off his shoulder and swiped at some frosting on my nose. "The inventory is on

7

your desk, and the cooler has been prepped and swept out. Can I go home now, mommy?"

"More like taskmaster," Amber sang helpfully from the front where she was cleaning out the empty trays from the bakery case.

I darted into my office, setting the bag of cash down on my desk. The inventory form was indeed sitting there in all of its glory, and I picked it up, reading over it with a practiced eye. I'd owned The Fluffy Cupcake for eight years, so inventory was second nature to me now. Brady had only been doing it for two years, but what I read had me scratching my head.

I lifted my gaze to Brady, who lounged in the doorway, one leg kicked over the other, and his toe resting on the floor while he waited. I hated the way he looked at me like I was a chocolate chip cupcake with chocolate buttercream icing. It unnerved me, but more than that, it sent a chill of excitement through me. The excitement part didn't unnerve me as much as it scared the crap out of me.

"We have next to nothing in the cooler?" I asked, surprised. "How did that happen?"

I tried to shove past him to check the cooler, but he grasped my shoulder and held me in place. "Haylee, you've been in your own little world recently. I don't know where that is, but it's not here with us. Are you okay?"

My mind raced straight up the stairs to my apartment and the calendar hanging on the fridge. The big red X loomed in my vision while the heat of Brady's hand burned through my chef's coat. The faces of all those guys I'd dated this past year converged until the only face I saw was Brady's. Secretly, the only face I wanted to see on those dates was his, but that could never happen for a multitude of reasons.

I swallowed and cleared my throat before I answered. "I'm fine. We've been busy, that's all. I'm trying to keep up, but admittedly, that's getting harder by the day."

His eyes told me that he knew I was lying, but he didn't push the matter. I was glad since I didn't need everyone to know how pathetic I had become. It was bad enough that Amber knew.

"Sure, okay," he agreed, but I could read between the lines. His sarcasm was evident in those two words. "Anyway, we've sold so much product—"

"Which is a good thing," I jumped in. "Business is booming."

"I agree," he said calmly, his hand still on my shoulder, only now it was kneading it. I had observed Brady knead bread thousands of times, and now I understood why his loaves were always the best in the case. His hands were magic. "It's taking more raw ingredients to get the job done, though. My job is to tell you what we have, and that's what I did. We have enough for two days of our usual items, but that's it."

"Two days?" I asked incredulously. "What I ordered last time should have lasted another week, at least."

"Not when we're selling out of our product every day. That's not even taking the special orders into account. Business *is* booming, and it's time to readjust our plan."

A breath escaped my lips. "You mean it's time I start paying attention and stop burying my head in the cupcake batter."

He shook his head, his hair shifting under his hat like it always does. I knew the locks were soft and silky because I once had to use his hair to catch myself from falling off a ladder. He probably didn't appreciate having chocolate cake batter in his hair for the rest of the day, but all he said was he was glad I didn't fall and get hurt.

"That's not what you're doing. You're trying to stay afloat with all that cupcake batter, and you don't have time to micromanage everyone else's job the way you used to. It's time to take the training wheels off and let me ride," he said, his long lashes sweeping across his cheek when he winked at me.

Amber probably heard me sigh with girly pleasure all the way out in the main bakery. Dammit, I hate myself right now. Why do I let those thoughts even wander through my head?

"You're right. I hate that you're right, but that doesn't change the truth. Do you want to take over the ordering?"

Brady's brow went up in surprise. "Completely?"

"For the most part," I agreed with a nod. "You're the kitchen manager, so you're already in charge of the cooler. You've worked here long enough to know how I do the ordering, too."

"Sure do," he agreed with a nod. "I'm not new to this, but I also don't own the place. I'm not going to step on any toes."

"That's a first," I muttered.

"What was that?" he asked with a smirk, which told me he'd heard exactly what I said.

"Nothing, I was just saying that you're not stepping on toes if I agree to you taking over the job."

He rolled his eyes in plain view. "Sure, it totally sounded like that. If I've stepped on someone's toes in the past, tell me now so I can fix it."

He was so close to me that I could feel his breath on my cheek when he spoke. I rested my hand on his chest unconsciously, but the immediate heat that burned my hand had me pulling it back instantly. *If you don't want to get burned, Haylee, stay out of the kitchen.* "You haven't. Ignore me. I'm tired. Do you want to take over the inventory, or not?"

He nodded once. "Yes."

"Good. That will help me out. The first few times, we'll go over the order together before you call it in, and once you feel confident with it, you can do it yourself. Remember, you always have to make sure you have all of the ingredients for the special—"

"Specialty items that we might need at any time," he finished. My heavy sigh of resignation made Brady chuckle. "I've been around the block a few times, cupcake. At some point, you're going to have to trust me."

"That's probably never going to happen, Brady. The Fluffy Cupcake is my business, and I don't trust it with anyone."

Cupcake

His finger bopped the tip of my nose, and he winked. "This is yours and Amber's business, and you trust her to do what needs to be done up front. Trust me to do what needs to be done behind the scenes, so you can keep making all of those delicious treats."

"We'll start with the tentative agreement to let you take over the ordering and work up to trust in a few years," I answered smugly.

Brady's laugh was long, low, and sexy as hell. I hated that the first place my mind went was to the bedroom—with him in my bed wearing nothing but that chef's hat.

I cleared my throat and prayed my cheeks weren't the color of Red Hots. "I'll need to see that order no later than tomorrow morning if you're going to do this."

Brady threw his arm over my shoulders and walked me toward the prep area in the back of the bakery. He lifted an iPad from his prep bench and handed it to me. "Check away, Chef Cupcake."

My gaze drifted to the iPad, where my order forms were loaded and ready for submission to the company websites. My fingers scrolled through the order forms, and I was more than a little surprised to see he'd even ordered all of the extra ingredients we needed for the special orders that came in today. After a few minutes, I lifted my gaze back to Brady's.

"You're my hero," I whispered, relief filling me that I didn't need to spend three hours here tonight putting the order together.

All Brady did was wink.

Two

I strolled into my kitchen wearing my Minnesota Twins nightshirt that I'd had since the tenth grade. It was almost paper-thin and had a few chocolate ice cream stains, but nothing else that I owned was as comfortable for a warm summer night. I grasped the handle on the fridge, ready for a glass of wine after a long day, but the red X on the calendar caught my eye again. "You don't own me," I whispered, sticking my tongue out at the offending paper.

Unfortunately, that red X did own me. It taunted me, and I regretted having the idea to mark my thirtieth birthday that way. If I'd just left the box empty, I could walk by it forever and pretend it didn't exist—the same way I'd done for the last twenty-nine years. That was much harder to do when it had a giant red slash through it.

My head fell back until I was staring at the ceiling. I'd been doing this for six months now. The whole point of the red X was to motivate me to make time for a personal life. The last eight years my sole focus had been on the business and it was time to change that. It was time to find my soulmate. I'd dated with gusto since January second, but so far, I'd struck out. All of the guys I'd dated thus far could barely tie their shoes.

There'd been Tim who had significant commitment issues to the point he couldn't decide if he wanted chicken or beef tacos. Then there was Shawn, who spilled his beans on my pants and spent the rest of the date telling people I'd pooped myself. Most would think that date would hold up in the record books as the worst, but they hadn't met Jerry yet.

I shuddered and blocked him from my mind. All the guys I dated this year taught me one thing. Sometimes, a vibrator is all a girl needs to mind her business. "Alexa," I said, waiting for the voice to fill the small apartment.

"What can I help you with today, Henlee?"

I rolled my eyes so hard it hurt my brain. I'd given up on getting her to say my name correctly after the first year. "Add a new calendar to the shopping list."

"I'm sorry, Henlee, you previously added a calendar to your list of not allowed items. Would you like me to remove it from that list?"

I sighed heavily.

"I did not understand your response, Henlee."

"Alexa, stop," I muttered, opening the door and grabbing a giant bottle of prosecco.

Pouring a glass, I stuck my tongue out at the red X. Mature, right? I didn't much care. I was exhausted, and another long day of baking was already lined up for tomorrow. Since tomorrow was Sunday, our hours were limited, but I had special orders to get ready for Monday morning. It was the beginning of June, and that was prime tourist and wedding season in Lake Pendle. If I didn't stay on top of things, I'd crash and burn faster than a race car with three tires.

As much as I hated to admit it, without Brady, I'd be screwed. He had worked at the bakery for almost seven years now and was a talented baker in his own right. "If only he didn't constantly call me cupcake," I muttered, lowering myself to the couch and grabbing the remote. A glass of wine and a little bit of Netflix would relax me enough to get some sleep before heading back to the bakery at four a.m.

The doorbell rang, and I glanced at the clock. It was almost eight o'clock, and I didn't order any food, though my brain suddenly decided that pizza would be welcome. I

Katie Mettner

sighed at my glass of wine and hoisted myself off the couch. With an eye stuck to the peephole, I saw the distorted image of my best friend. She waited impatiently on the postage-stamp-sized landing at the top of the long stairway to my apartment. I opened the door and was immediately greeted by a warn nighttime breeze that rustled Amber's hair.

"What's wrong?" I asked, grabbing her arm and pulling her into the apartment.

"Nice to see you, too," Amber said, laughing. "Nothing is wrong. I just thought I'd come over for girls' night. Is that a problem?"

I grinned, and laughter filled my voice when I spoke. "Not a problem at all. You just usually call or text, so I was concerned. Do you want a glass of wine?" I motioned at mine sitting on the table, and Amber nodded exaggeratedly.

"You get that. I'll order a pizza. I'm feeling prosecco and Northwoods Pizza with pepperoni and green olives."

I gave her the thumbs-up and headed back to the kitchen for the bottle of wine and another glass. Suddenly, I was glad for the unexpected company. The loneliness building deep inside my soul was getting out of control, and I spent too much time at the bakery just to avoid being at home alone. It wasn't healthy, but at the same time, I didn't want to bother my friend with my issues all the time. Lord knows I have enough of them, and she had dealt with them enough over the years.

I had lived with Amber and her family for the last three years of high school. As a foster kid, I moved around a lot, but the one constant in my life had been Amber and her family. If I hadn't found that stability during the last few years of my teen life, I might not be as successful as I am today. Amber was like a sister to me, and I knew she'd listen, but I felt like at almost thirty I should be able to be alone for more than a few hours without feeling that sinking sense of depression. Lately, that was all I was feeling.

Cupcake

I closed the door of the fridge, and my eye caught the red X again on the calendar. With the wine and glass in my hand, I muttered as I left the kitchen. "You don't own me."

The problem was, it did.

"That was an okay movie," Amber said when she flicked off the television.

"If you like cheesy romance movies about coffee shops," I agreed. "Which I do, of course."

Amber laughed and pointed at me before refilling her wine glass. "You've always been a closet romantic. Hard candy coating on the outside, gooey on the inside."

I forced myself not to roll my eyes at my best friend. "Sometimes, you have to be tough. Life can be hard."

We sat in silence and thought about the truth behind that statement. We both knew just how hard life could be. Amber had an idyllic home life, but she suffered every day physically after an accident broke her leg, arm, and ribs. She once told me she'd take all the broken bones in the world if it meant she didn't have to keep watching me suffer at the hands of my foster families. That's why I know she was the one to convince her parents to become my respite foster parents. They took me in one weekend a month to give me a break from the hell I lived in the rest of the time. When her oldest sister graduated from high school, her family took me in full-time and offered a stable environment for me to heal my heart a little bit before I became a jaded adult with no direction.

Once I graduated from high school, I found my salvation in a little bakery in St. Paul. I worked there every morning while I went to school at Saint Paul College for culinary arts. After being trained in all aspects of the kitchen, my true love remained with the pastries. I used to joke that my hips and ass proved it, but the last year has stolen that phrase from my lips, too.

"I heard you made an executive decision today without consulting your partner," Amber finally said, tapping the stem of her wine glass on her thigh.

My mind snapped back to the conversation, and I tipped my head to the side. "About?"

"Brady taking over the ordering."

"Oh," I said, taking another swig of wine. "I'm sorry, I should have told you, but you're still in charge of the ordering for the front of house items. He's only doing the kitchen side of it."

Amber rolled her eyes to the ceiling and shook her head slightly. "That was sarcasm, Hay-Hay. I'm not upset about it. Hell, it's about time you started delegating a little bit of the work. If Brady knew anything about what I do up front, I would happily let him do my ordering, too, but he doesn't. Before you know it, we'd have forty boxes of donut bags and no bakery papers."

I grinned but hid it behind my wine glass. "Accurate. Honestly, my decision today was rash, but after a few hours of thinking about it, I can see it was necessary. I'm spread too thin right now. I'd be stupid not to utilize the talent we already have in place."

"So you're saying Brady is talented," Amber joked, pointing her glass at me.

I had to bite back a smart retort because she'd take that as weakness immediately. "I'm saying Brady has worked at The Fluffy Cupcake for seven years. He can manage the added responsibility as long as he keeps his head in the game instead of thinking about his latest conquest."

Amber grunted and waved her hand. "You have an elevated sense of how many women he actually dates. Regardless, his head is in the game."

"It sure felt like it when he showed me the order form this afternoon. He didn't do it exactly the way I do, but in the end, the order was correct. He even noticed things I didn't, like how much more candy we're going through. He also found a better price on sugar. He did some complicated mathematical equations to predict how much extra flour, butter, and eggs to have at different times of the year, too. I can't complain about his thoroughness."

"Well, frost my head and call me a cupcake," Amber said, the wine making her giggle at the thought. "Haylee Davis had something nice to say about Brady Pearson."

"Hey!" I exclaimed, holding up my finger. "I always give credit where credit is due. That doesn't mean I'm going to date the guy."

"You could, though," Amber said instantly. "He's been trying to take you out for years."

"Correction," I said on a huff. "Brady has been trying to get in my pants for years, which frankly, I still don't understand. Why does he want to date someone like me when he's taking out blonde-haired, blue-eyed models every night of the week?"

Amber finished the wine in her glass and set it next to the empty pizza box. "He's not. Again, that's just this thing you've made up in your head about him. He wants to date you because you're a chestnut-haired, brown-eyed curvy beauty with a big brain. You put those other women to shame."

I grasped her hand and squeezed it, the only way I knew how to acknowledge the compliment. "Thanks, but it's more like I'm a thick chick he's never going to look back at after he bangs me. Don't worry. I'm not going to sleep with him and ruin the dynamic we have going at The Fluffy Cupcake." Maybe a change in subject was in order before Amber decided to marry Brady and me off to have little cupcakes of our own. "I can't believe how much the business has grown since we opened eight years ago. Do you know that we only have enough supplies for two days? What I ordered last week would have lasted two more weeks just a few years ago."

Amber's eyes bugged out, and she leaned forward, bracing her elbows on her knees. "Are we going to be okay? Do we need to make a run to Costco?"

I waved my hand at my neck. "We'll be fine. Our truck will be here Tuesday, so it's no problem. I knew we were going through a lot of product, and I wish Brady had come to me sooner with the information. It's his job to stay on top of inventory."

"He was," Amber said, lifting a brow, "as evidenced by him coming to you today. If I know Brady, and I do, he figured you'd need to see a depleted inventory sheet before you'd believe him. You tend to ignore a lot of what he says, and poo-poo his ideas before you give them any consideration. I can't say I blame him for adding a little shock factor this time. At least you finally listened to him."

"I don't poo-poo anyone's ideas!" I exclaimed, sitting upright on the couch. "That's not fair!"

Amber lifted a brow in response. "We know you don't do it intentionally, and we all know why you do it, but that doesn't mean you're not missing out on great ideas to grow the business or make your life easier. It's been especially bad this year."

My head fell back against the couch, and my eyes closed. Amber was probably right. I did poo-poo ideas that didn't jive with my plans sometimes. Not all the time, but when I did, the poo-pooing usually involved Brady Pearson.

"I'm tired," I whispered. "Thinking about or adding new ideas to an already overflowing baker's bench stresses me out."

"And pretending everything is fine, doesn't?"

I opened one eye and pinned it on Amber. "No, but it does allow me to get up every morning and get through the day."

"I've heard of better coping mechanisms," Amber muttered.

I nearly choked while trying to hold in my laughter. As if Amber had any right to talk about coping mechanisms. I finally sat up and clasped my hands in front of me. "How about we have a meeting tomorrow afternoon? I'll make a batch of peppermint bonbon brownies, and we'll even invite Brady. We can hash out ideas, make changes that will improve business and customer flow, and see how we can change things to take a little bit of stress off everyone's shoulders."

Amber sat up and threw her arms around me. "I think that's a great idea," she whispered. "For you most of all. I'm afraid when the clock flips to midnight on July thirteenth, and you see that red X on your calendar, you'll think your life is over."

"Don't be silly," I said, ending the hug and nonchalantly waving her off. "My life isn't over just because I'm single when I turn thirty."

Amber's head bobbed on her shoulders as she considered what I said. "I guess what I'm saying is, you've lost focus on what's important. Instead, what focus you do have, is on that red X. You've been obsessing about that for the last six months instead of enjoying all the success you've earned over the last eight years." She stood and held up her finger. "You know what? I forgot for a moment that I have the power to change that."

She stomped off in the direction of the kitchen, and before I could catch up, she'd ripped the month of July off the calendar and ripped it into shreds.

"Amber! What are you doing?" I shrieked from the end of the counter, as she made confetti out of my calendar.

"I'm helping you refocus. The idea that you need to find a man by your thirtieth birthday is ridiculous, Haylee," she said, sweeping the tiny white pieces into her hand and stomping to the bathroom. She tossed the paper into the toilet and flushed it with aplomb. "There. Officially refocused."

My mouth opened and closed several times without words coming out. "But—but, how am I supposed to know what day it is?"

"Alexa, what day is it?" Amber asked, waiting patiently.

"Today is Saturday, June first," Alexa said.

"Problem solved," she answered, her hands up in the air.

I sighed and shook my head at the woman leaning against the wall of the bathroom. "No, the problem is most definitely not solved," I whispered, my head in my hands. "That red X was a goal, Amber."

She put her arm around my shoulders and walked me back into the living room. I sat on the couch and she refilled my wine glass. "It wasn't a goal, Hay-Hay. It was an albatross around your neck. Love doesn't happen because the calendar says it's time. Love happens when the moment is right, and the person you're with makes you forget about the days on the calendar."

I brought my glass to my lips and drained it. Amber may be right about that, but the bigger picture was one I couldn't let anyone see. I lowered my head to my hand and grasped my forehead. I had already found the person who made me forget about the days on the calendar, but dating him was out of the question. Nothing sucked more than working day after day with the guy you're in love with while knowing you can never be part of his life. Amber might not understand that, but I did, all the way to my crushed and mangled soul.

Three

The scent of peppermint wafted through the bakery, now empty other than the three main players in the business. While Amber and I have several part-time workers that help in the front of the bakery, they weren't included in this discussion today. In truth, I didn't have to include Brady, considering he wasn't a partner in the business, but he was integral to what we do here, and his ideas always held merit. He's intuitive when it comes to the small changes that can make things so much easier. We've already implemented a lot of those ideas over the years, so having him here for today's discussion made sense.

I made a strangled snorting sound and rolled my eyes. Sure, whatever you need to tell yourself, Haylee. Brady might be a playboy, but he had magic hands. He could get the most stubborn dough to do what he wanted, and the same could be said about women. Brady was great at coaxing young, sweet, dopey girls who made puppy dog eyes at him into his bed. Okay, that's not fair. All of the girls probably weren't dopey, unless they were dopey in love. The rest was completely accurate per the Lake Pendle gossip mill.

Cannot confirm one hundred percent, though.

When I hired Brady, he was fresh out of school in Milwaukee and looking for a new life. I wasn't convinced he was aching to live and work in a town the size of Lake Pendle, though. With a population of eight thousand in the summer and far less in the winter, we weren't exactly a metropolis. After growing up in a city the size of Milwaukee, I worried we'd give him a serious culture shock. Brady took the job nonplused by the idea, and I expected him to last a year here before he went in search of more opportunities in a bigger city. Now, seven years later, he was still here baking bread and keeping my butt in line. Ironic, since I was supposed to be his boss. Then again, keeping my butt in line wasn't easy when you factor in the size of it. I laughed out loud at my joke and then glanced around to make sure no one was within earshot. They didn't need to know that the boss was falling apart at the seams.

Every year, I bake a special cupcake on the anniversary of each employee's start date to honor that person. I only make that cupcake once a year, so everyone races here in the morning to get one before they are gone. Brady's was a light, airy peanut butter cupcake topped with buttercream icing and a mini Pearson's Nut Roll. He started working here on July twelfth, and that meant his seventh anniversary was coming up soon. Customers were already asking if I was going to have Better than Brady cupcakes, which is what I called them in jest, again this year.

I always swallowed around the lump in my throat and told them I would, but I was also secretly holding my breath. Every year, until the day of his anniversary, I wondered if it would be the year he turned in his resignation letter and headed out for bigger and better things. I worried about that until the morning of July twelfth when he stood at the workbench, helping me decorate twenty dozen cupcakes. He would laugh his wonderfully deep, rich laugh as he settled the nut roll on the top of each one. He pretends to hate the premise of the cupcakes, but I know he secretly eats it up. As soon as the bakery opens, he's at the bakery case with Amber laughing with the locals and passing out cupcakes to anyone looking for a fix.

That was what made it hard to hate Brady Pearson. As much as he got under my skin about my personal life, he knew his trade. When he wasn't baking or keeping the cooler in order, he was researching new products, organizing community events, and schmoozing with the ladies when they showed up for their morning coffee and pastry.

It was always a struggle for me to admit, but Brady was an essential part of this team. It was time I acknowledged that. It might kill me to do it, but I had to— for him and me. I set three cups of coffee down on the table then grabbed the new catalogs that had come in the mail yesterday. If we were going to do this, we might as well do it right, even if it took all night.

"Hay-Hay!" Amber said, darting back into the bakery. She plopped down in a chair and let her heaving chest catch up with her breath. "You're never going to believe this."

I slid into a seat next to her and put my hand over hers. "Are you okay? Do you need some water?"

Amber's head swung wildly. "I'm fine." She wiped her brow with a napkin, and the breath from her lips ruffled her bangs. "I was trying to run. You know how this leg is sometimes." She motioned at her stick-thin leg wrapped in a large brace.

"I do, but why were you trying to run?"

"Two reasons. The first was, I didn't want them to see me. The second was, I had to get back here and tell you!"

I made the *out with it* motion with my hand. "Tell me what?"

"I just saw Jerry Hill and Darla McFinkle in a lip lock in front of the bank!"

"You have got to be kidding me," I said, my lip turned up in a sneer.

Darla McFinkle was my sworn archenemy. That's not even a dramatic statement. We've been at odds since the first day of kindergarten. I still don't know why Darla acts the way she does, but she loves nothing more than to poke at me every chance she gets. I started giggling, and soon it was full-on laughter. "She thinks I'm in love with Jerry Hill, so she's dating him!"

We fell across the table, our shoulders shaking with laughter and our snorts of pure amusement filling the small room.

Slowly, I sucked up air to catch my breath. "If Darla only knew how much I don't love Jerry Hill. I should feel bad that she's sucking face with that vampire in an attempt to make me jealous, but I just can't get there with it."

"I hope he doesn't leave fang marks!" Amber said between giggles. "He's so creepy." An involuntary shiver racked her body while she made a gagging sound. "Sorry, I just thought about kissing Jerry Hill and almost vomited."

"Who's kissing Jerry Hill?" a deep baritone voice asked from the doorway.

I sat up and straightened my coat unconsciously when Brady walked into the room. More like he commanded the room. I hated that he had that kind of presence wherever he went. Okay, I didn't hate it. I loved a man who could work a room and immediately join in on a conversation to move it along. That didn't mean I had to like that he was one of them. It was just another notch on his side of the board that I was forced to ignore.

"Darla McFinkle," I answered when he sat down in the empty chair between us.

His lip went up in a sneer of distaste. I guess no one liked Darla in this town. I bet even a disgusting excuse for a human being like Jerry Hill didn't actually like her. Then again, they were perfect for each other. Maybe Lake Pendle had a new love match. I rolled my eyes at myself for being so snarky.

"They kind of deserve each other," Brady said, snagging a brownie and taking a bite. The moan he released while he chewed made me instantly wet. All I could think about was that sound in my ear as he made love to me.

Stop it, Haylee!

24

Cupcake

I squirmed in my seat, refusing to make eye contact with Amber or Brady. Right now, all they'd see was a sex-starved twenty-nine-year-old woman reflected in my eyes.

"Good God, Haylee. These are incredible. I hope you made enough for tomorrow. They're going to fly out the door when people get a whiff of them. How do you get them so moist and rich?"

"She uses homemade bonbons," Amber answered, lifting one from the plate. "See," she pointed to the tiny bonbons sliced clean through by the knife. She didn't wait for him to answer, she just took a bite and closed her eyes, savoring the crème de menthe when it hit her tongue.

"I would make these a staple in my diet, but then I'd have to spend another three hours at the gym every week," Brady agreed.

I huffed at the two of them. "I'm glad you like them, but it's just a brownie. We make much more complicated confections here than peppermint brownies."

Brady brushed off his hands and took a swig of coffee to wash down his treat. "Something doesn't have to be complicated to be top-shelf, Haylee. Finding flavors that complement each other in a simple, non-complicated way, always makes for a winning combination. Don't forget that."

I couldn't help but think the same was true about life and love. Complementing each other's strengths and weaknesses in the business made us successful at The Fluffy Cupcake. As for complementing each other's strengths and weaknesses in the bedroom, well, I was now going to try and stop thinking about that before I couldn't concentrate on anything else.

I put my hand on the catalogs and took a deep breath. "Okay, we're here for a reason. It's time to strategize. We've done great already with weddings and special orders this year, but we have several more events to go, including the Lake Pendle Strawberry Festival."

Brady pointed at me. "We should start there."

Amber agreed while she swiped another brownie. "July tenth is only a month away, and you haven't even told us what the cupcake would be for the bake-off."

"It's a closely guarded secret," I said, shaking my head. "You know that."

"True, but if I'm going to help you, I need to know what it is," Brady reminded me.

I blew out a breath at the thought of him helping me at the bake-off. I spend every day baking with Brady, but the festival atmosphere always changed the charge in the air. It was going to be so much temptation working that close to him for hours. He was all male from his perfectly styled blond hair, his chiseled cheeks covered in a tightly capped beard, and a gym physique that didn't quit. He had muscles in places I didn't know you could have muscles. I glanced down at my less than muscular body. Some would say I was fluffy. Some would say the nickname fluffy cupcake fit me to a T. Well, at least Darla McFinkle thought it did.

My hips loved cupcakes, and my ass loved Brady's artisan sourdough. Since I hated working out and got most of my exercise running around the bakery, lifting heavy pans of cupcakes out of the oven, and walking up and down the thirteen stairs to my apartment, that didn't help my non-bodybuilder physique. In hindsight, my choice of professions may not have been the best one for my body type. C'est la vie, as they say

"Haylee?" Amber said, and I snapped my head up to stare into their confused faces.

"Sorry, I got lost in my thoughts for a second there."

Brady was staring at me with intense concentration as if he could see right through me and into my soul. Like he could read my thoughts and know that I was lusting after him like a dopey girl making puppy dog eyes. It was making me uncomfortable, and I wanted it to stop. I grabbed the iPad and opened the photo app, moving the brownies aside so I could set it in the middle of the table.

"I give you the fluffiest of fluffy cupcakes." I motioned at the image like Vanna White, revealing twenty-five thousand dollars.

Two heads leaned into the table to stare at the image on the screen.

"Stats," Amber said without taking her eyes off the iPad.

"Time to make," Brady added, his assessing gaze sweeping across the cupcake in a way that kept me hot and bothered in a way I liked far too much.

"A strawberry cream cheese cupcake, filled with a light strawberry crème filling, topped with a whipped strawberry sorbet icing, and garnished with a cream cheese stuffed strawberry dipped in chocolate."

Brady sat back and rubbed his hands together. "Oh, it sounds like a winner to me."

Amber agreed with a nod since she was chewing on another brownie already.

"How are you going to make a sorbet icing, though?" Brady asked. The confusion in his voice was evident as he thought about the heat of a July day.

"I won't be making it out of sorbet, but it will taste like sorbet. I'm going to make a test batch this week, and you can tell me what you think."

Amber raised her hand and waved it around wildly, dragging a laugh from both Brady and me with her silliness. He rested his hand over mine for a second and leaned down to make eye contact. "It's already a winner in my book. I know the judges will feel the same way, cupcake."

I fought hard not to roll my eyes at the man sitting next to me. His constant habit of calling me cupcake was disrespectful as my employee, but no matter how many times I asked him to stop, he never did.

"It's going to be stiff competition this year," Amber said, sipping from her coffee mug. "Darla is entering the bake-off, too."

This time, I did roll my eyes. I rolled them so hard Brady grabbed the back of my head.

"Don't lose those beautiful brown eyes back there," he ordered possessively.

I swallowed before I responded, hoping my voice didn't shake when I spoke. "Oh," I said, waving my hands in the air, "look at me shaking in my boots with fear. Do you think Darla will ask Jerry to be her assistant?"

Amber almost choked on the swallow of coffee in her mouth. "I hope not. You don't want to look at his creepy face all afternoon."

Brady dropped his hand to rest in the crook of my elbow and glanced between us. "I dated Darla for about two and a half seconds, and I can promise you, you have nothing to worry about."

Amber and I recoiled in horror. "You what now?" I asked, my voice filled with venom. "You dated my archenemy?"

Amber and I leaned in, waiting for his answer. He leaned back and held up both hands in the don't shoot position. "It was before I knew of your history together. A guy I knew set us up when I first got to town."

"Why haven't you mentioned this before?" Amber demanded, her disgusted tone of voice saying volumes.

He motioned at the two of us without words.

I held up my hand, and we leaned back to give him space. "Fair point. I just can't imagine anyone willingly dating her."

"I only went to avoid upsetting my friend. I was new to town, and he was trying to help me out, but I knew she wasn't my type."

"Not your type?" I repeated, and he nodded. "She's five-ten, one hundred and ten pounds, blonde-haired and drop-dead gorgeous. I had her pegged as your exact type."

"I'm not into girls who are high maintenance," he said, savoring another bite of brownie. "I also prefer women who are a little bit," he motioned around with his hand, "less made up, have a little meat on their bones, so they don't poke me with their hips, and have something between their ears other than cotton balls, if you know what I mean."

Amber and I bit back our laughter at his parting shot. "You're saying Darla is a scarecrow?"

"Let's just say the date ended for me when she thought Jane Austen was a dress designer."

Amber crumbled in on herself with laughter, and I had to cover my mouth to keep from doing the same, but my eyes radiated glee. "I'm not laughing at you, I swear. I'm laughing at your accurate assessment of Darla."

He held up his hand and shrugged. "All I can say is, I hadn't been in Lake Pendle long, so I claim a lack of knowledge of the landscape and its people. Of course, Darla always acts quite put out whenever she sees me now."

Amber waved her hand at him. "Doesn't matter. Darla is put out by anyone not willing to put her on a pedestal and carry her around."

I sat up and shook out my arms. "Okay, enough about Darla. Are you ready to hear some new ideas for the bakery?"

Amber and Brady rubbed their hands together and nodded. "Wow us," Brady said with jazz hands.

Nervously, I brought out the first catalog, which was dog-eared on several pages. I didn't know if I'd wow them, but I'd be happy if I could convince them that my ideas would be worth the extra work in the long run. More than all of that, when I opened the first dog-eared catalog page, and Brady's eyes lit on the products, I hoped he'd understand that I saw him as a valuable part of the team here. Maybe I couldn't say those exact words, but we needed him at The Fluffy Cupcake.

Sometimes, seeing is believing, right?

Four

I took a deep breath and knocked on the door of Haylee's office. When she glanced up, her eyes told me she was more than a little surprised to see me.

"Hey. I thought you went home."

"I did," I said, stepping into the small space. I glanced down at my black tech shirt as Haylee's eyes roamed over my chest, taking in my hard abs in something other than my chef's coat. I could see the appreciation in her gaze, and I liked it. I liked it a lot. "I was going to the lake and thought you might like to go, too. We could sit on the dock and drink this," I said, holding up a six-pack of craft beer.

"Tempting," she agreed, her brow in the air. "Extremely tempting, but it's late, and I have to be back here to start baking in a few hours."

I leaned against the door frame with my shoulder and lowered my brow at the woman. She was way too gorgeous and way out of my league, but I didn't care. I hadn't given up trying to convince her otherwise. "It's only eight. It's still light outside. One beer, and then I'll walk you home. You work too hard, cupcake. Sometimes you have to take a break before you burn out."

"I prefer to think of it as keeping my business alive," she joked, but she stood from behind her desk at the same time. She wore a pair of hip-hugging denim shorts that made my groin tighten instantly. This woman was going to be the death of me if I didn't figure out a way to make her mine. I'd taken so many cold showers over the last seven years I didn't even need a hot water heater anymore. "I suppose I have time for one beer before bed."

I offered her my famous Brady Pearson smile. "Excellent. It's a beautiful night out, and it would be a shame to waste it locked up in the bakery."

Once the lights were shut down and the business was locked up, we strolled toward the lake and the large, public dock that stretched out into the water. It was a favorite place for the locals to hang out on a warm, sunny day. Some liked to fish from it, some wanted to take a running start and dive off the end, and some just wanted to sit on the wooden boards and take in some sun.

Tonight, I wasn't interested in the dock, the lake, or the view, unless you counted the picture-perfect view beside me. I struggled to keep my eyes in front of me instead of on Haylee's gauzy blouse that billowed in the night breeze. Every time her ivory shoulders peeked out, they teased my senses with the suggestion of what else I would find if I ever pulled that shirt off her beautiful body. It was rare to see Haylee Davis in anything other than her white chef coat with her hair pulled up in a tight ponytail and covered in a very unsexy hairnet.

That wasn't the case tonight.

Her gorgeous chestnut hair was down and bouncing against her shoulders with every step she took, the natural body of it curling against her neck. Haylee Davis made Little Brady stand at attention every time she moved for the sole reason that she was who she was. Between the gauzy blouse, the sway of her hips, the way she cared about everyone she worked with, and her gigantic brain I couldn't hold a candle to, I was utterly smitten with her. I also felt like a teenage boy trying not to get a boner in the middle of math class when my crush walked up to the board to work out a problem. I'd be working out my problem tonight— alone in the shower. I moaned softly at the thought of how much better it would be to work out the problem in her bed together.

"It's a beautiful night tonight. A little sticky, but it is June," she said as we approached the dock. I turned left away from the public space when I noticed how many people were still hanging out there. I should have predicted it would be that way in early June when the air was finally thick with summer. Haylee hurried to catch up and grabbed the sleeve of my shirt. "Where are you going? The dock is back there."

I cleared my throat before I spoke, so my words didn't sound garbled. The heat of Haylee's hand burned against my arm and made me think about what it would be like for her to touch me in other places. "Too many people. I don't want to share the beer," I joked, holding up the case again.

I noticed this time it was Haylee who swallowed hard. Her beautiful, long, sleek neck bobbed once before she stuttered about for words she couldn't find. "But there's no place else to go."

Slinging my arm around her shoulders, I winked at her. "That's where you're wrong. I know this great little spot, right up there," I explained, pointing at a small patch of sand on the shore of the lake.

"Are you sure that's not private property? I have to work in the morning. I can't spend the night in jail for trespassing."

I grinned and motioned for her to go ahead of me. It was purely selfish. If she was in front of me, I could watch the sway of her hips. It was pure torture and pure bliss at the same time. I groaned at the thought of those muscular thighs wrapped around my waist while I brought her to orgasm.

Fuck, man. You have to dial it back a few hundred notches. She's your boss and your friend. You're worse than that horny teenage boy in math class.

When she turned back, I coughed and plastered a smile on my face. I already had half a hard-on and her delicious bottom was going to make it a whole one in ten more seconds.

"You're right, it is private property, but I know the guy, and he told me I was welcome to use it whenever I want. It might be the size of a postage stamp, but at least it's private."

I helped her sit down on the sand and sat next to her, handing her a beer after I twisted the top off. We clinked the necks together and sipped the hoppy liquid in the warm night air. The sun was thinking about setting, and the sky was turning brilliant reddish-orange in the sky. The light reflected on the water until a boat broke the image for a moment. Idyllic was a good word for the sight before us.

"Lake Pendle is so idyllic at this time of day. The epitome of a small-town lake community," she said, lowering her beer to the sand.

"I was just thinking the same thing," I agreed, shaking my finger at her. "Being from Milwaukee, which is anything but a small town, this view always captivates me."

Not as much as her body captivates me all day, every day, but I wasn't going to mention that. I valued my job and my balls too much.

Haylee tipped her beer bottle at me before taking another drink. "I was just thinking today how surprised I was that you stayed in Lake Pendle. I didn't think you'd last long here before you moved on."

"Almost seven years now, and I have no intention of leaving, Haylee." My arms stretched wide across the space in front of us. "What's not to love about this?" I'd play off the lovely town before I'd admit that the reason I stayed was her.

Her head was nodding when I tuned back into the conversation. "I agree, but I grew up here, so I stay for different reasons. Most city slickers can't find enough to do here, especially in the winter."

I shoulder bumped her carefully and winked. "My boss keeps me too busy in the winter to worry about things to do. It's bread, bread, bread, day in and day out."

She chuckled, and the sound cut right through me. Her laugh was a faint melody that reminded me of wind chimes on a warm summer night. "She sounds like a real bitch. Can't believe you keep working for her."

My smile grew, and I wrapped my arms around my knees to keep from touching her. God, how I wanted to, but I was smart enough to know she didn't want me to.

"You know—it pays the bills." I shrugged, and she bumped me in the shoulder with a smile on her face.

"If that's all it does, you should probably find something more fulfilling."

I bit back a groan at the thought she'd be more fulfilling if I were filling her. Dammit, man. You have got to get your libido under control. She's your boss. You've devoted seven years to your craft at The Fluffy Cupcake. You can't risk that stability to scratch an itch. "As it turns out, she's slowly warming to my sourdoughs and rye."

Haylee's brow lifted when I handed her a second beer. She hesitated, but finally accepted it and took a drink. Her left hand patted her ample thigh. "I've loved your warm sourdough and rye since the first loaf came out of the oven. After seven years, I think that's made obvious by my one size bigger work pants."

I had to bite my lip to keep from thinking about her work pants. I wanted to take them off and discover what was underneath. As it was, keeping my eyes on the lake and not on the way she caressed her thigh was hard enough. Speaking of hard. I was.

"At the risk of overstepping work boundaries, let me assure you, your work pants are perfect."

We sat in silence while the sun continued to set, tossing the lake into shades of orange, yellow, and pink. My mind drifted to the meeting this afternoon and the changes she suggested. They had taken me by surprise, and I needed a few hours to think about it before I could ask any questions. I was more than curious about why she was doing this now, though, when she'd been resistant to change for years.

"So, you're serious about the new displays?" I asked, finishing the second beer and setting it back in the cardboard to take home with me.

"I wouldn't have said it if I wasn't, Brady."

Cupcake

"I guess it took me by surprise because you've always maintained that The Fluffy Cupcake was a cupcake shop, not a bread shop."

"That may have been true when you first started at the bakery, but as with everything in life, things change. Your breads have added to the landscape of the business, and some days, we sell more bread than we do cupcakes. The new wicker and wire displays will showcase the beauty of them better than we can now by keeping them behind the counter. They make new wrapping to keep the bread crusty and still protect the loaves from germs and handling by the public. That was always my biggest hang-up. Now that I can protect the product, I think it's a win to do it."

I nodded, my gaze still on the lake. "You don't mind giving up the tables you'll need for the displays?"

Haylee's hands weighed back and forth in front of her. "Everything is a tradeoff, Brady. While we'll lose a couple of tables where people can sit and visit, I don't think that will make a huge impact. I plan to put those few tables outside during the summer months for the tourists to use. We don't have a ton of regulars who sit in the bakery during the winter, so I don't see a problem with it. The benefit is, the customers can pick out their own loaves rather than the front worker always having to deal with it. It streamlines things, especially during the summer months."

"All excellent points," I agreed. "It also allows for impulse buys. People are more likely to buy a couple of loaves when they are in control of picking them out."

She wore a smile on her beautiful face when she answered. "You're right. We've seen that with the packaged goodies, too. The display cases are beautiful works of art, but when people can grab a couple of different pre-made packages of cupcakes and check out without waiting in line for help, they tend to buy twice as much as they otherwise would. I'm learning to make changes where I see they need to be made. It's slow, but I'm learning."

I couldn't stop myself when my hand came down on her back to rub it up and down a few times. God, she was warm and soft. The longer we sat together, the more her jasmine perfume teased my senses into overdrive.

"I don't know anything about how to run your business, Haylee, but I think you're doing great. I can bake bread, but you do it all."

She tossed her head back and laughed in a way I had heard only a few times in the seven years I worked at The Fluffy Cupcake. The first time I heard it was on the first anniversary of my hire when she brought out the nut roll cupcakes and saw my reaction. The sound went straight through me and lodged somewhere in my chest. I hated that she didn't laugh like that more often, and I always wondered why. She was reserved and quiet most of the time. It was only on a few occasions that she let her guard down enough to show me little peeks of the real Haylee Davis.

"You underestimate yourself, Brady. I know we knock heads a lot in the bakery, but that's because we both have strong personalities. We have strengths the other doesn't, and that's why we work together so well, even when we're pelting each other with bread dough."

"You're saying I'm indispensable then?" I asked jokingly, and she immediately leaned into me, her laughter filling my head again.

"I'm saying that without your added talents over the last seven years, The Fluffy Cupcake wouldn't be where it is today. Both Amber and I know that. We were nervous bringing someone on who was an unknown to us and the town, but over the years, you've proven yourself to be valuable and dedicated." She stuck her finger in my chest and gazed at me from under her brows. "And if you tell anyone I said that, I'll deny it until my dying breath."

I smirked but didn't remove her finger from my chest. She was touching me, and I didn't care where or how, as long as she was. "Mums the word," I promised, zipping my lips and tossing the key into the water.

Haylee's hand fell to the sand, and she sighed as she gazed out over the lake. "I suppose I should head home. I'm on for baking at four a.m. tomorrow."

Cupcake

I pushed myself up off the sand and offered her my hand. "Me, too. My boss, I tell you," I grumped, rolling my eyes.

That same laughter I loved so much filled the air again, and I bit back the moan of pleasure it shot through me, especially when she slipped her hand into mine. I hoisted her up, and she brushed the sand off her pants. It was innocent, but it shot a white-hot poker of desire to my groin.

I was going to need that cold shower sooner rather than later.

Five

I snapped the collar straight on my polo shirt and smoothed it down over my hips. I was already late for the date I didn't want to go on, but Amber wouldn't let me cancel. Okay, so technically, I was meeting him in fifteen minutes. Canceling would be rude, but that didn't mean I didn't want to—especially after spending Sunday night drinking beer on the beach with Brady. I hated that I liked it as much as I did, but I also couldn't deny it. There was no way a guy like Brady Pearson was interested in anything more than a business relationship with me. Maybe a friendship at the most. Besides, I didn't want anything more from Brady Pearson, right?

I let out a loud *ha* and shook my head in disgust. I'd had to remind myself of that the entire time we worked at the bench together this week. He was always brushing by me and innocently caressing my shoulder or smiling that playboy smile of his when he thought I wasn't looking. I was always looking, which I kind of think he knew and was using to his advantage.

We'd come to a truce about the business, deciding that working together was smarter and more natural than fighting against each other's ideas. That was where this truce ended, though. Brady was all power, heat, and male sexiness that I wasn't prepared to wrangle. It would be like a baby tiger trying to take down a fully grown elephant. It wasn't going to happen.

I flicked the bathroom light off and decided a guy like Tieg Tulip I could wrangle. He was about to pick me up for my twenty-ninth date in my twenty-ninth year of life. I had no illusion that it was going to be the date of a lifetime. I gave it better than a fifty-fifty chance that it would also be the last date of my twenty-ninth year of life for two reasons. His name was Tieg Tulip, and Amber was the one who set us up. Amber might be my best friend, but she would never make an excellent matchmaker.

I grabbed my purse, and a light sweater from the kitchen table then locked the door behind me. I had no intention of letting Tieg know that I lived above the business. I'd done that one time in the past, and it took weeks of ignoring someone knocking on my door to get them to stop. If I didn't hit it off with Tieg, and let's face it, I wasn't going to, I didn't want him to know where I lived.

Sure, he'd know where I worked, but then everyone knew that. Guys usually shied away from making a scene in a public place, too. They preferred private space for that. I rolled my eyes thinking about the fit Jerry had thrown when I finally had to spell out for him just how disinterested I was in dating him. He was one of the few bright ones who figured out that I lived above the bakery and had climbed the stairs one night while half-drunk to knock on my door. I still don't know how he made it back down the stairs while drunk and angry without breaking his neck, but somehow, he had.

"Well, if it isn't the fluffy cupcake," a sugary sweet voice said from behind me. I sighed. Great, as if things weren't bad enough with Tieg Tulip, now I had to deal with McFinkle.

"Darla," I said dryly, leaning up against the front of the bakery. "A delight, as always."

"I hear you'll be doing the cupcake bake-off again this year," she said, her nose turned up in distaste. "I think it's getting a little worn."

"You may think whatever you'd like, Darla." This woman was getting on my last nerve. She could have opinions, but I was tired of always being at the brunt of them.

She flipped her hair haughtily and stuck her nose up in the air the way she always does. "Won't matter. This year, I have the winning recipe. I hope you're ready to get the pants beat off you. Not even the fluffy cupcake, you, not the business, can top this. It's going to be epic."

"I look forward to the competition," I said, no emotion in my voice whatsoever. Darla could tell me that the sky was green, and I would say she was right. I learned at the ripe old age of six not to trust her or to argue with her. Darla has to be right about everything, and I wasn't going to be her punching bag more than I already was.

She hiked her bag over her shoulder and sneered at me. "Maybe you should let Brady be the face of the business at the bake-off instead. He's more, what's the word," she motioned her hand around as though searching for the proper way to express herself, "visually appealing than you are."

"That's two words, Darla."

"Two words that describe that fine specimen to a T. I would worry if I were him that those hips and ass of yours swinging around could just knock those cupcakes right off the table."

"I'll make sure to send him the memo."

With her nose in the air and a stick up her ass, she strolled down the street, not even caring that she just ruined my night. I shook out my shoulders and pushed off the wall of the bakery. No, I won't give her that power. Whenever she comes around calling me names, my mood always plummets, and I couldn't keep doing that. I was getting better about not engaging with her in an antagonistic way. I had to get better at controlling the way her words hit me, too. It would never be easy, but in the long run, it would always be worth it.

A man strode up the street dressed in a short sleeve dress shirt, open at the collar, and a pair of dress shorts.

My gaze strayed to his feet, relief filling me when he wasn't wearing sandals with socks. He was wearing perfectly acceptable black Nikes—score one for Tieg Tulip.

He pulled himself up short in front of the bakery and thrust a bouquet of, yup, you guessed it, tulips, out to me. "Haylee, I presume?"

I accepted the tulips and smiled. "Tieg, I presume?"

"Of course, who else would bring tulips?" he asked, as though I was a tulip short of a bouquet.

Off to a good start.

I pushed back the eye roll threatening to escape and offered a smile instead. "Who else, indeed. I'll put these in the cooler inside, and then we can head out?"

"Oh, no," he said, shaking his head. "You can bring them with us. That way, everybody knows I'm a gentleman."

Blink. Blink.

I was infrequently at a loss for words, but Tieg Tulip had managed it in our first two minutes together. Propelled along the sidewalk by his beefy mitt, I struggled to find something to say to put the night back on track.

"Amber says you're a science teacher?"

"Ag-science," he corrected, as though I should know there's a difference. "I teach small animals and dairy science besides my duties running FFA."

"Exciting," I said with fake enthusiasm, even though it sounded a lot like watching paint dry to me. "As a baker, I don't know where I'd be without my farmers and their fresh eggs and milk."

"You'd be working somewhere else," he answered logically.

I bit back a sigh and plastered a smile on my face. "Without a doubt. So, where are we going for dinner?"

"We can eat at a restaurant any day, right?" Tieg asked, and I got a sick feeling in the pit of my stomach. "I put together a little private picnic at the lake instead. You won't believe the goodies I've got in my basket."

I was pretty sure, considering our already bizarre conversation, that I would believe it. I was also sure I wasn't going to be a huge fan of said goodies.

I strolled through the park on the way back to my apartment but paused halfway through, wondering if that was Haylee sitting at a picnic table near the community dock. I tipped my head to the side in fascination. Was that a bouquet of tulips stuck between the slats of the table? She sat across from a guy who looked like the love child of sasquatch and an Abercrombie and Fitch model. Curious, I walked closer, glad the guy had his back turned to me.

When I got a little bit closer, I could see it absolutely was Haylee sitting there with some sort of bento box in front of her. Whatever was going on, her hunched shoulders told me she wasn't enjoying herself. Her eyes met mine, and what they said had me strolling over to them.

"Oh, hey, Haylee," I said casually. "I didn't know you were out and about tonight."

The look of relief on her face told me I'd read the situation accurately, even from thirty yards away.

"Brady!" she exclaimed with a little too much excitement. "What a surprise."

"Beat it, buddy," the guy said, swatting at me like a fly. "We're on a date."

My gaze flew back to Haylee, and she was mouthing *save me*, her eyes filled with desperation.

"I'm sorry to interrupt, but I was looking for Haylee. There's a problem at the bakery. I need your help," I said to her, "or we might not be able to open tomorrow."

The guy across from her snorted like a feral hog. "I'm sure you can handle it with all of your muscles."

I balled my fists at my side and inhaled deeply to keep myself from punching this guy. I didn't know who he was, but I wasn't playing tonight. "I don't own the bakery, Haylee does. It's her call on how the oven gets repaired." I turned and addressed her, hoping she understood there was nothing wrong with her expensive bakery oven. "It won't heat when I turn it on. Just sits there and clicks."

She stood instantly, and the dramatic nature had me believing she was frantic. "That's not good. Not good at all. If we don't have the oven, we can't bake that special order for tomorrow. Oh, brother." Her hand was at her throat as she acted her way into the record books. Haylee turned to the guy across from her. "I'm sorry, Tieg. I will have to address this. I'm sure it will take all night. Thanks for the lovely picnic. It was nice of you to go to all the bother."

Haylee practically grabbed my hand to get away as fast as possible, but Tieg stopped us in our tracks.

"You forgot your tulips!" he exclaimed, thrusting them at her and going in for a kiss that was inappropriate in the current setting—or ever, for that matter. I had to bite my tongue to keep from telling him to back off.

I grabbed Haylee's waist and diverted her around the guy, a growl on my lips while I did it. I propelled her down the street toward the bakery, one hand at her waist and the other plucking the tulips from her hand and tossing them in a garbage can.

"Who was that guy?" I asked, slowing our pace and releasing her waist now that we were far enough away from the beach.

"That was the twenty-ninth date of my twenty-ninth year of life. It was also my last date forever and ever amen. I'm never dating again."

I bit back my laughter, figuring it wise to listen to her rather than make fun of her. "What about the tulips?"

The sound she made was a cross between a snort and a gag. "His name is Tieg Tulip. He wanted me to carry them around with us during the date, so people knew who gave them to me."

"Where does Amber find these guys?" I asked in confusion. "I assume Amber set you up."

Haylee held her arms out. "Oh yes, and she wouldn't let me cancel when she sprung it on me last minute."

"There are a few bits of good news here, cupcake," I assured her when we reached the bakery.

"I sure hope so because the last hour has been nothing but pain."

I unlocked the door and ushered her in. "The first bit of good news is that there isn't a thing wrong with the oven."

She wiped her hand across her brow and sighed. "Definitely good news."

I led her toward the back of the bakery and motioned her toward the bench. "The second bit of good news is, you just eliminated one more guy that you don't want to marry."

She burst out laughing. It was the kind of laughter that made my groin react instantly. God, she was stunning, and all of these dopeheads didn't even realize it. "That is the best news of all."

My finger went up into the air. "Actually, the best news of all is that we're both free, it's only six-thirty, and we have the bakery to ourselves."

"For?" she asked perplexed.

"A trial batch of the newest fluffy cupcake. Strawberry cheesecake sorbet."

She grabbed an apron off the hook and tied it around her waist, a smile plastered on her face. "I like the way you think, Brady Pearson. Let's get our cupcake on!"

The high five I gave her before I jogged to the cooler was in place of the kiss I wanted to plunk on her sweet, plump, kissable lips. One day, I would find a way to kiss Haylee Davis without getting slapped, so I'd bide my time with cupcakes—for now.

Six

I licked the frosting off my fingers and grinned at the man across from me. "So?" I asked, the mess around us ignored while I waited for his verdict on the cupcake.

Brady moaned low in his throat, and the pleasure written on his face said eating my cupcake was as orgasmic as making love was. I bit back laughter. Eating my cupcake. Was that some subconscious Freudian thing? Probably.

It was the fluffy part of the equation that reminded me why a guy like Brady would never eat my cupcake. I had to stop saying that! Guys like Brady don't date women like me. I was left with guys like Tim, Jerry, and—gag—Tieg. Those were the kinds of guys who didn't mind the fluffy part of the equation. Well, except Jerry and Tim and Tieg. Ugh. Never mind. They all mind the fluffy part of the equation. Tieg mentioned the size of my hips more times in an hour than I cared to remember. I set the cupcake down, my appetite gone at the thought of his thinly veiled reminders about my weight.

Brady's eyes opened, and all of that deliciousness pinned me to the bench. "We're going to win. Hands down. I don't even need a second bite. These are..." He made the mind-blown motion with his hand. "Forget Strawberry Cheesecake Sorbet. We're calling them Berry Sinful."

"Berry Sinful, huh?" I asked, a brow in the air. "This is only the first batch. I bet we can make them even better before the competition in a few weeks."

"Doubtful," he said, around another bite. "Fluffy, the perfect amount of sweetness, and the icing is like a puffy cloud when you bite into it." His eyes rolled back in his head when he took another bite.

"That's the marshmallows," I said, making a note on the pad next to me. "I'll make sure to keep it as part of the recipe. We get one secret ingredient. Do you think the marshmallow is worthy of being undeclared?"

Brady pointed at me with his mouth full of cake. "If you let Darla know you're using it, she'll jump on that bandwagon."

I put a star next to the marshmallow crème. "Done. The last thing I need right now is to be beaten by Darla McFinkle. My life would be over. She stopped by earlier tonight. You know, before the date with the loser, because if my night wasn't already bad, dealing with Darla just added to the pleasure. Anyway, she's convinced she's going to beat us, so we better bring our A-game." I rolled my eyes to show my sarcasm, and he rolled his back at me.

"Her winning would be a hit to your baking prowess. I'll give you that."

"No, it would be the end of my baking career. I'd never pick up another beater again. I'd curl up in a ball and rock in the corner until the earth swallowed me whole."

His brow went up, and his lips followed in a smile. "If I didn't know you as well as I do, that sentence might make me think you're a bit of a drama queen."

I chuckled and rested my ample hip on the baker's bench. "When it comes to Darla McFinkle, I just might be."

He waved his finger around in the air at me. "What's your beef with her?"

"Have you met her?" I asked dryly.

"As stated, I took her out on a date. She was full of herself, but—"

I pointed at him. "That's my beef with Darla. She's so full of herself that there's no room for anyone else in her atmosphere."

Brady shrugged. "I've learned one thing when it comes to women like Darla. She's not full of herself. She's actually about the least confident person I've ever met, and she knows it."

I huffed, rolled my eyes, gagged, and pelted the cupcake in the garbage. I didn't need it anyway. It would only add to the fluffy part of me.

He chuckled and shook his head. "That was a lot of drama right there."

"Because you clearly don't know women," I said, starting to clean up the bench. "If you did, you wouldn't have just defended someone's archenemy to their face."

I stomped around the bakery, dumping the garbage, binning the rest of the berries, and packing the cupcakes in a box for tomorrow. We had made a small batch, and I'd save the rest for Amber and everyone else to try. If they all liked them as much as Brady and I did, we'd have a winner for the competition. I hadn't planned to bake the first batch tonight with him, but it worked out, I guess. Usually, I liked baking the first batch by myself. That way, if they flopped, no one was the wiser. I had enjoyed myself being able to bake with him in a relaxed atmosphere. Too bad he had to go and ruin it by defending Dumbass Darla.

Brady grabbed my arm on one of my mad dashes past him. "Haylee, I wasn't defending her. I was just explaining my impression of her. I'm not saying you have to agree with me. She has a way of rubbing people the wrong way. I don't deny that. I cross the street to avoid her, too."

My shoulders deflated, and my anger quickly dissipated. "I get defensive when it comes to women like Darla in all their skinny, made-up glory." I waved my hand at my neck. "Forget it." I grabbed the box of cupcakes and headed to the cooler. "I'll save these for Amber to try. Hopefully, she likes them as much as we did."

"She will," he said when I joined him again at the bench. "You know cupcakes. You don't need her approval, or mine, to know they're winners."

"True, but I still want people to love them. I want them to come to The Fluffy Cupcake looking for more."

He leaned his strong forearms on the bench. "I've never asked how you came up with the name for this place. Something tells me it wasn't for the simple reason it's catchy."

I clapped my hands together and headed to the light switches. "I think it's time for bed. We're only six hours away from being back here again." He grabbed my arm before I got to the door, and I sighed internally. I didn't want to be alone in the bakery with him, but I was also glad I wasn't alone with Tieg. I'd take Brady over tulip boy any day. "Thanks for saving me from that horrific date tonight, Brady. I appreciate the lifeline since I couldn't get a text out to anyone."

"It wasn't a problem, Haylee. I could tell you weren't enjoying yourself, for whatever reason. Now it's time to stop dodging my question. It shouldn't be that hard to tell me why you picked the name for your business when I ask."

I pursed my lips and wiggled them around a bit. "It's bottom-line basic, Brady. I picked the name because cupcakes are fluffy. It made sense."

He didn't let go of my elbow. "I'm not blind, cupcake. I saw your reaction the instant I asked that question."

"Don't call me cupcake!" I said, wrenching my arm free of his hand. "Men, you're all the same!"

"How are we all the same?"

"You don't listen, and you won't take no for an answer!"

"Whoa, back up the cupcake wagon. Did some guy not take no for an answer, Haylee?"

I huffed and crossed my arms over my chest. "I haven't met one that has yet. Some have been worse than others. There were some where I wasn't sure if I was going to get out of the situation unharmed, which is another reason why I appreciate your help tonight. I suspect Tieg Tulip wouldn't have taken no for an answer, that is, if he could get past the size of my hips and ass, which…" I made the so-so sign in the air with my hand. "Didn't seem likely considering he mentioned the size of them no less than two dozen times." My shoulders deflated, and I leaned on the baker's bench, my chin dropping to my chest. "I know you're new to Lake Pendle, but Darla has been after me since the first day of kindergarten. Defending her to me is like claiming store-bought bread is just misunderstood."

Brady's laughter should have been infectious, but I was too tired to join in. I was tired of the day, but even more tired of my boring life. Life with Brady would at least be entertaining. That was as likely to happen as Darla deciding to stop bullying me.

He rested his hand on my shoulder lightly, and I didn't move away, which took me by surprise. Maybe I was just too tired or in need of a little comfort, no matter who offered it.

"Listen, I get what you're saying. I was just trying to make you feel better about Darla nagging on you all the time. I'm relatively new to the town in the respect that I didn't grow up here. I didn't know the history between you two ran that deep. Forgive me?"

"Nothing to forgive," I said, before pushing off the bench. "I always overreact when I'm tired. Especially when it comes to Darla McFinkle."

Brady hung his apron on the hook and slung his arm over my shoulders while we walked out the front door. "I'll take you home, but for the record, the size of your hips and ass is size perfect. Don't let some loser make you think otherwise. I'm warning you now, Haylee Davis, someday you will tell me why you named this place The Fluffy Cupcake."

I locked the bakery door and tucked the key in my pocket. Walking backward toward the stairs on the side of the building, I held my hands out at my sides. "I am home, and it shouldn't be that hard to figure out. Night, Brady."

I climbed the stairs to my apartment, fatigue making my feet heavy with each step. Brady's laughter carried through the quiet night air and filled my head with ideas a girl like me shouldn't have. Size perfect hips and ass or not.

Amber stood at the bench, snarfing down a cupcake at five a.m. Her moans filled the bakery, and the sound of lip-smacking was all you heard besides the constant whirl of the oven where more cupcakes rotated in all of their baking glory.

"Hay-Hay, these are seriously the cupcake of the century."

Rolling out a pie crust on the bench, I bit back a laugh. "Amber, it's just strawberry cake batter. It's not up for a Pulitzer."

"You're right, they're up for Lake Pendle Strawberry Festival Cupcake of the Year, and these are the ones. You're going to win hands down." She tossed the cupcake paper in the trash and brushed off her hands.

"The only time I've ever lost was when I didn't enter," I said, laughter in my voice. "I'm glad you like them. That's three for three."

Amber's brow went up in curiosity. "Who else tried them besides you and me?"

"Brady," I answered nonchalantly. "He helped me bake them last night. You should have heard him. He was as bad as you with all that moaning, oohing and ahhing." I checked the clock. "I wonder where he is. He should be here by now."

"He probably overslept after spending so much time last night making cupcakes with his cupcake."

My fist came down on the wooden bench with force. "I am not his cupcake! And it wasn't that late."

Cupcake

Amber held up her finger in confusion. "Why were you baking cupcakes with Brady instead of on a date with Tieg. That was last night, right?"

The deep inhale of air through my nose told her she was about to get an earful. "Oh, it was last night. Tieg Tulip is indescribable when it comes to how truly awful he is."

"I take it you two didn't hit it off?" Amber asked, leaning her ribs on the baker's bench. She was so short she needed a stool whenever she had to work on the bench with me. It aggravated her when we teased her about using the kiddie stool.

"Hit it off?" I asked, slowly setting the pie aside. "No, we didn't hit it off. He was rude, didn't listen, mentioned the size of my hips in a derogatory manner too many times, and insisted I carry his tulips around town as a reminder to people that he was the one who gave them to me."

"Seriously?" Amber asked, her lip curling up.

"You know me. I don't sugarcoat anything. I was at the park having a horrific time at a picnic with him when Brady came along. Thankfully, he noticed my discomfort and rescued me from the situation."

"Brady rescued you from a date?" she asked in shock.

My hands went out to the side. "We were having a picnic in a public place, and Brady saw me sitting there. Tieg was none too happy about him interrupting, but I owe Brady a debt of gratitude. I can't say for sure what this guy was going to try at the end of the date, but I do know I wouldn't have liked it."

"Damn, I'm sorry, Hay-Hay," she said, taking my hand. "I knew he was a bit odd, but sometimes oddness is endearing. Obviously not in this case."

I squeezed her hand and then released it to get back to my pies. "If I were you, I wouldn't help Tieg find dates anymore. You'd hate to feel responsible if he did something to one of your friends."

Amber's hands went up in the air. "Agreed. I'm scratching him off the potential suitors' list. I guess date number twenty-nine was a bust."

"Just like the dates one through twenty-eight were," I agreed with my head nodding. "I'm done dating now. I can't deal with these guys. They all think they know everything, all they want is a woman to control, and thus far, none of them have had any respect for the fact I own and run my own business. They're either too caught up in themselves, or too caught up in my measurements."

Amber's frown told me she wasn't in the same camp about giving up on love. "Hay-Hay, you can't give up. Besides, I know someone who admits he doesn't know everything, doesn't want to control a woman, has the utmost respect for you owning your own business, and he's hot to boot."

Brushing a strand of hair off my face, I paused in the filling of my pie. "Well, where is this mythical unicorn?"

"Coming in the back door," Amber said.

Before I could react, she spun on her heel and flounced to the front of the bakery to load the pastry case. The sound of Brady's humming from the back room filled the bakery, and my heart contracted. He might be all those things, but he would never be mine.

Seven

I set the last of the cupcakes down on the freezer rack and let out a sigh. It had been a long hot day, but the work was finally done. Now I could go home and catch up on some missed sleep. I was working more now than ever, and I knew my latest change in the bakery personnel had been the wrong one.

The idea had frosty white plumes puffing out into the cold air where I stood. I had initially hired Brady as my kitchen manager and part-time baker. He worked his way up to making all the bread, buns, and now the ordering, which was great. The problem was, I was already regretting that decision. He was too talented as a baker to have him squired away doing inventory. He should be at the bench as a full-time baker. He'd been working toward it for years, and when I made a rash decision to put him in charge of inventory, I did it out of fear. I was too afraid of working with him full-time to offer him the position. Now, I worried Brady was offended that I overlooked his work at the bench. Knowing Brady, that wasn't likely, but *I* knew I made a mistake. It was a mistake I'd have to rectify.

First, I would have to talk to Amber about who would replace him as our kitchen manager. Secretly, I hoped she would tell me I was crazy to promote him, and then I could leave things alone. Truth be told, I wasn't sure I could work at the bench with Brady full-time. It would be a lot harder to keep my roving eyes and hands to myself if I had to work next to him all day every day instead of just a few hours a day.

I pushed open the door to the freezer, deciding to deal with it another day when I wasn't tired, hot, and hungry.

"There you are!" Amber said, throwing her arms up in the air. "I've been looking all over for you."

"Sorry, was finishing the last of the cupcakes for tomorrow's order. What's up, buttercup?"

Amber tapped her watch impatiently. "You heading upstairs to change. Chop-chop. You've only got an hour."

My eyes rocked back and forth in my head while I searched the database for what I had forgotten. "An hour for what? I'm going to bed. I've been up since three a.m. It's Sunday, and I need a nap."

With my pink and white frosting stained apron tossed in the bin, I spun on my heel to head for the door, but Amber grabbed my arm. "Not so fast, petunia. You have brunch with Maxwell in an hour at The Modern Goat."

My head swung in denial instantly. "Not in this lifetime or the next one will you find me having lunch with Maxwell at The Modern Goat. I don't even know who that is," I exclaimed, throwing my hands up. "I told you, no more blind dates!"

"I had this one set up before you told me that, though," Amber insisted, pouting the way she used to when she didn't get her way when we were kids. "It's too late to stand him up now."

The growl that tore from my lips would have put a rabid dog to shame. "And you waited this long to tell me because you knew I'd cancel!"

"Maybe Maxwell will be your soulmate. If you stand him up, you'll never know." My best friend gave me a frowny face and batted her lashes at me. "Besides, this date will make it an even thirty for your twenty-ninth year of life. If you don't hit it off with him, I promise I'll never set you up on another blind date."

"Where do you find these guys anyway?" I asked, heading for the front of the bakery. "Do you surf dating websites looking for the biggest losers in the area and then hook them up with your loser friend?"

"You are not a loser!"

I flipped the open sign to closed and spun back to face my oldest friend. "If that's true, then why do you keep setting me up with losers?" I paused and held up my finger. "And why aren't you dating these guys? Why do you keep setting me up with them?"

Amber huffed and crossed her arms over her chest. "I'm happy where I am. You, on the other hand, are not, so I'm doing what best friends do and helping you find someone."

"Best friends bring booze and pizza to movie night. They don't set their best friend up for failure with every loser in town."

"Maxwell isn't from town," she said, chasing after me as I headed for the back door. "He's from Dawsbury."

I huffed and rolled my eyes, grateful she was behind me and couldn't see me as I started climbing the stairs to my apartment. Dawsbury was the next town over, there were less than one thousand people in that village, and all of them were farmers. I love my farmers, they keep me in eggs and butter and everything else I need to make cupcakes, but I have no desire to date any of them. "Great, you want me to date a guy who smells like manure and wears teat dip as cologne!"

Amber's finger twirled around my face when I turned. "You're kind of picky."

I tossed my arms up in the air again. "I'll go on the stupid date, and I'll give your farm boy a chance, but this is it. Do you hear me? The next time you set me up with someone, I will break the date, and I'll never talk to you again!"

"You're the one who wanted to be in a serious relationship by thirty!" Amber exclaimed. "I've been trying to find you a guy, but you're constantly finding something wrong with all of them!"

"That's because every single one of them points out all my flaws on the first date! I'm never dating again. I'm happy being alone if every available guy is as awful as the ones you've set me up with so far. Keep this up, and I'll start finding you guys to date who are equally as terrible!"

The threat made, I slammed the door and bolted for the shower. Maxwell might smell like manure, but I wasn't going on a date smelling like sweat and sickly-sweet frosting. When I climbed in the shower and lathered up, I only felt slightly bad for yelling at my best friend. Amber was right when she said I wanted to be in a relationship by thirty. I just had no idea how impossible of a goal that would be when I made it.

I was never going to find a single guy who wasn't an asshole in this town. When I closed my eyes to rinse the soap from my hair, the blue eyes of one Brady Pearson filled my mind and reminded me not every guy in Lake Pendle was an asshole. I just couldn't date the only one who wasn't.

The Modern Goat was reasonably busy, so I asked to be seated on the patio. Besides the obvious benefit of being able to enjoy the beautiful day, if Maxwell did smell of manure, the fresh air would allow me to eat without gagging. Also, if he turned out to be as bad as the other twenty-nine dates were, the patio allowed me an escape route back inside to ditch and run.

"Can I get you something to drink?" the hostess asked after she seated me.

"A Goat's Beard Tea would be fantastic," I answered, hooking my purse on the edge of my chair.

The hostess assured me it would be right out, and I leaned back in the chair to wait. I had no idea what Maxwell looked like, so I'd have to guess, which could be kind of fun. Chances were good he'd be wearing a ballcap from the feed supply store, work boots with mud still on them, or a John Deere t-shirt. Some might say I'm jaded, but I'd dated enough to know what was going to happen here today. That's why I decided to go with a Goat's Beard Tea. It was nothing more than a Long Island Iced Tea that they renamed to fit the venue. The tourists loved the kitschy names, even if the locals rolled their eyes.

The other benefit of The Modern Goat's patio was the view of the lake. If nothing else, I could enjoy a few drinks and a nice meal while watching the boaters on the lake. Once I exhausted my incredibly shallow well of small talk with Maxwell, I'd escape back to my apartment and sleep until tomorrow morning.

"Haylee?" someone asked from behind me, and I turned, coming face-to-face with a guy in a western shirt and jeans.

I stood to shake his hand, and my eyes drifted to his feet.

Work boots with mud.

Then his head.

Ballcap from John Deere.

I fought the snicker that wanted to burst from my lips. Did I know Dawsbury or what?"

"You must be Maxwell," I said, shaking the hand he had extended. "I'm Haylee."

His grip was firm, and his smile was wan. "Otherwise known as The Fluffy Cupcake."

I bit the inside of my cheek, so I didn't overreact. "No, my business is known as The Fluffy Cupcake. I'm just Haylee."

We sat, and the hostess brought my drink, stopping and asking Maxwell what he would like. After he ordered a Budweiser—shocker—he settled in while I sipped my drink. "Have you ordered yet?" he asked, checking out the trendy menu of farm to table choices The Modern Goat was known for in the region.

"I was waiting for you," I said while he read over the menu. I didn't even have to look at the menu, I knew it by heart. Every few seconds, I noticed his eyes check me out over the top of the paper before they'd dart back to the printing again. Seriously, I want to know where the heck Amber finds these guys.

The waitress set his draft beer down and pulled out her order pad. "Are you ready to order?"

Maxwell answered before I could. "I'll have the blue goat burger with fries." His eyes roamed over me and stopped at my hips. "You said you wanted the raspberry chicken salad, right?"

I sucked in air at his words. Where in the hell does he get off implying I need to eat a salad instead of a burger? Setting my jaw firmly, I glanced up at the waitress. "I'll have the blue goat burger with fries as well, thank you."

Our waitress, Sara, a girl I'd gone to school with, smiled a smile that said she knew exactly what was going on. "I'll put your order in. Would you like a side of fresh cheese curds while you wait?"

"Oh, yes," I said gleefully at the same time Maxwell said no.

Sara twirled on her heel and skipped off to put in the order while Maxwell frowned. "So, tell me a little bit about yourself," he said, his fingers toying with his beer glass. "What do you like to do for fun?"

I finished my first drink and motioned to Sara to bring a second before I answered. I was going to need a lot of booze to get through this date. My head was already swimming from the first one, but since I was walking home, I didn't care. "Amber and I are real movie buffs. We love sitting on the couch with a bottle of wine and a pizza to watch old eighties films. I don't have a lot of free time with running the business, so I have to prioritize what I want to do when I'm not working or sleeping."

"I see," he answered, nodding while looking anywhere but at me. "How about exercise? Do you like to ride a bike or run?"

"My exercise involves running between the baker's bench and the oven twelve hours every day," I said, my tone as sharp as a pin.

Cupcake

Sara arrived with the cheese curds and drink, setting both down and winking without a word. I grabbed a curd and blew on it, popping it into my mouth before holding the basket out for him. He shook his head, his lips in a thin line.

"I'm not into fried cheese," he said after a sip of beer.

"That's a shame. Fried cheese is the best. Wisconsin knows what they're doing over there," I said, eating another one and washing it down with my drink. Amber was so going to pay for this. I was going to show up on her doorstep with every asshole guy I could find in a tri-county area. Okay, so I wasn't, but I wanted to, and that's what mattered.

"I don't believe that your life consists of baking, sleeping, and movies. There must be something else you enjoy. Do you swim, or are your legs that size from all the running in the bakery? What about your family?" he asked, digging in to make the date something it would never be.

Successful.

Ignoring the comment about the size of my legs was extremely difficult, but I refused to stoop to his level. "I lived in foster homes my entire life. My parents abandoned me at birth, probably because of the size of my legs."

Okay, maybe I wasn't going to ignore it. Moving on.

"No one even knows who they are. My family consists of Amber and the other people I employ at the bakery. You?"

His throat-clearing told me I'd surprised him with my honesty. "Wow, that's a lot to deal with at your age. I had no idea. I live on our farm with my parents. Always have, always will."

I finished my second drink and grasped my purse. "Would you excuse me for a moment? I need to use the ladies' room."

He motioned for me to go ahead, without getting up, and I darted into the restaurant and up to Sara, who was plating our food. "Hey, Sara. Would you put mine in a box?"

Her grin was wide while she did what I asked, then handed it over. "Want me to deliver his burger like nothing is amiss?" she asked, the tray in her hand. "I'll tell him yours isn't quite done, and I didn't want his food to get cold."

I gave her the thumbs-up sign. "Perfect. If Max stiffs you on the bill, give me a ring, and I'll run over and pay for it."

"Girl, no one stiffs me on the bill—especially not jerks like him. Go, before he catches on. I'll let you know how it turns out."

I chuckled and winked at her. "You're the best! I'd say have a good day, but you're not going to until he leaves."

Sara motioned for me to go, and I dodged out the side door, having to walk the long way around to get back to the bakery. I didn't care. Besides, walking this way allowed me to stop by Amber's house. I was going to ask her what the hell she was thinking setting me up with that jerkoff. Then I was going to ask her if she would consider hanging up her matchmaking gloves forever.

Eight

When Amber opened the door to the pounding of my fist, she didn't look happy. She rubbed at the sleep in her eyes and yawned. "The date seriously can't be over already."

I pushed my way inside and plopped down on the couch. "The date ended before it even started. Want a burger? I'm not hungry."

Amber took the box and opened it, inhaling the delicious scent of beef and blue cheese. "Why do you have a burger in a to-go box, and where is Maxwell?"

She ate the burger while I filled her in on what happened. When I finished the story, Amber sighed and set the box down, offering me a hug. "I'm sorry, he's a friend of a friend. I don't know him more than in passing. Are men really that big of pigs these days?"

I nodded and pointed at her. "Most are bigger pigs than Max was."

"Not all, though. Brady isn't a pig. I happen to know for a fact that he wouldn't mind if you poked his loaf."

The sound I made was a half-drunken snort. "He's been trying to get me into bed for years, Amber. It's a game. We both know it. He doesn't want me to *poke his loaf*," I said, using air quotes. "Besides, I'm his boss, and that's not happening. Why don't we have booze and cupcakes?"

Amber snickered and pushed herself up off the couch. "I know just the place for the cupcakes, and I bet I know where we can pick up some booze. Let me change."

While Amber was in her bedroom, I leaned back on the couch and pinched the bridge of my nose. The disastrous last six months of the year played out behind my eyes—all the dates that went wrong, and the few guys that lasted a week or two before they ditched my giant ass. I was hit with the knowledge that my idea to find someone to love me for who I am before I turned thirty had been a bad one. What made sense to me on December thirty-first had become an albatross around my neck the closer I got to July thirteenth. The revelation brought me to the only decision I could make. I had to let it all go. I couldn't force something to happen if it wasn't meant to happen. That was a lesson I should have learned before I went on thirty dates from hell.

When Amber returned, we left the apartment and stopped off at the local store for a bottle of vanilla cupcake flavored vodka, and a bottle of strawberry wine, then unlocked the back of the bakery to feast on some cupcakes while we drank.

I was chewing a wonderfully decadent chocolate cupcake when an idea hit me. I threw my hands up in excitement. "Oh! I just had the best idea ever!" I set my cupcake down and ran to the cooler, gathering supplies before I dumped it all on the bench.

Amber gazed at me in a drunken stupor. "What are you doing? Why can't you be normal?"

"I am normal. A normal baker!" I dumped ingredients into the small mixer and set it to mix while I grabbed a measuring cup and poured half a cup of vodka into it. I held it up like a trophy. "Vanilla cupcake vodka cupcakes!" Unceremoniously, I dumped the liquor in and let it mix while I measured flour, salt, and soda.

Amber's laughter rang out through the bakery while she lined a pan with papers. "That's a lot of cupcake in one name. We need something catchier. Also, can we sell cupcakes laced with booze?"

Cupcake

I didn't know, and I didn't care. I was already busy scooping the mess into the pan and shoving it in the oven. "Sure, we will call them the cupcake for the twenty-one and over crowd! They'll fly out of here like hotcakes. If they taste good, that is." I dumped butter and powdered sugar in a bowl and started the mixer again, dumping in more vodka and letting it spin. "Maybe it is illegal to sell alcoholic cupcakes." I waved my hand. "No matter. If we can't sell them, I'll make them for us to eat behind the scenes!"

"What are you making now?" she asked, motioning at the mixer.

"The frosting. Duh," I said, but the words were starting to slur from all the booze I'd swallowed in the last few hours. I hadn't eaten anything, either. Wait. Do cupcakes count as food?

While I made the frosting, Amber disappeared into the main bakery and came back with a loaf of pepperoni cheese bread. She sliced it into large wedges and buttered it, pushing a piece toward me.

"You need to eat that. Your words are starting to run together."

"I don't want to poke his loaf," I said smartly, shutting the mixer off and leaning on the bench.

"I didn't say poke it. I said, eat it. Geez, what is your problem lately?"

Rather than answer, I shoved in half the slice of bread and chewed, moaning a little bit when I swallowed. "Dammit, why does he have to be so good at his job?"

"Because he cares about your business, his craft, and you," Amber answered, taking a bite of her piece of bread.

"That was a rhetorical question." I spun around and pulled the cupcakes out of the oven. I decided to pop them into the cooler at the last second, enjoying the sound of the slight sizzle when I set them down on the rack.

"I didn't think you were supposed to put hot cupcakes in the cooler like that." Amber pointed at the door with a drunken finger.

"Normally, I wouldn't, but these aren't normal times. I need them to cool so I can frost them and put them in my belly."

Amber's laughter filled the bakery, and I took another bite of the bread. "Well, at least you're excited about eating them. Usually, you eat a cupcake like it's a death sentence."

"Only to my hips, apparently," I answered. "At least according to Maxwell." Before she could say anything, I decided to go for gold. "I was thinking about something and wondering what you'd say about it."

"If it's about sleeping with Brady, then my answer is yes," she said, leaning on the table and finishing her bread.

I shoved her playfully in the shoulder. "It's not about sleeping with Brady!" I said with laughter in my voice. "It is about him, though."

"Damn. Here I thought all the booze helped you see how perfect he is for you."

"First of all, Brady Pearson is not perfect for me. He's the exact opposite of me."

Amber's finger trailed through the flour on the bench for a few seconds before she spoke. "That's not true, but you're the only one who doesn't see it. You and Brady aren't that different. You just don't want to admit it. You don't like change, even when you say you want things to change."

"I do not!" I exclaimed angrily, my foot stomping on the bakery floor. "Wait. I do too!" I said, tipping my head to the side. "What was the question again? Oh! I do like change. That's what I wanted to talk to you about, but never mind now."

I turned my back to her and finished the bread, then checked the cooler to see if the cupcakes were ready for icing. They weren't. Dammit. Patience, Haylee. You are usually more patient than you have been over the last six months. What is wrong with you? It probably had something to do with the fact that I was tired, sex-starved, and unhappy in my personal life, or rather my lack thereof.

"I'm sorry, Hay-Hay," Amber said, coming over and putting her arms around my shoulders. "Sometimes, I don't think before I speak."

I sighed and shook my head slightly. "We both know I don't like change, and we both know why."

"I do, and I shouldn't have said that. What did you want to talk to me about?"

"Just bakery stuff," I said on a shrug. "I was thinking I screwed up with Brady offering him the inventory position instead of the full-time baker."

"He didn't seem upset to me when I talked to him. He was excited that you were putting more trust in him with the business."

"It was the wrong kind of trust, though. I realize that now. Brady's so good at what he does, and I could really benefit from him being at the bench with me full-time."

"You don't have to ask me about the back of the house hiring, Hay-Hay. We agreed that we hire for our own ends without requiring approval from the other person."

"We did, but this would require me hiring a new kitchen manager, at least part-time. I know Taylor is looking for more hours, but I can't offer the position to her without you okaying it."

"If that's what you want to do, then I say go for it. Taylor would be great at it. Increasing her hours also means she'll stick around, so that makes it a win-win-win."

"No, that makes it a win-win," I said, counting on my fingers in case I was too drunk to remember how many wins there were.

"Nope," she said, shaking her head. "A win for Brady, a win for Taylor, and a win for you for getting to work with Brady full-time. Win-win-win," she said, threw me a wink, and clapped giddily like she just solved world hunger.

Nine

I was late for a very important date. Okay, not a date, but I was still late. The team was going to have my ass in a sling if I even thought about stopping to talk to anyone. I didn't care.

"Haylee," I called, jogging up to the woman meandering down the sidewalk. When I got closer, I realized she wasn't meandering. She was listing.

"I'm not going to poke your loaf, Brady," she answered without turning around.

Poke my loaf?

"For once, you've left me speechless, cupcake."

"All evidence to the contrary," she slurred, her tongue sounding too big for her mouth. Was she sick?

I grasped her shoulder and held her in place. "Are you okay, Haylee?"

Her eyes rolled around in her head when she tried to focus on me, and I bit back laughter. She wasn't sick. She was drunk.

"Have you been tippling, cupcake?"

The punch to my gut took me by surprise. "I told you not to call me cupcake! And you claim that you know how to listen." She started stomping up the street, but the booze in her system made it more of a stumble than a stomp.

Cupcake

I put my arm around her shoulder and propped her up against me. "Do you have plans for the night?" I asked while I directed her toward the lakeshore.

"Big plans," she said, holding up a bag that I hadn't noticed tucked against her side. It was brown paper and most definitely held alcohol. "I'm going to drink this whole bottle of strawberry wine by myself. You can't have any."

With a brow in the air, I had to ask. "How many bottles have you already had?"

"I think one," she answered. "No, I shared that one with Amber. Wait, that was vodka."

"You've already had half a bottle of vodka?"

"It was a small bottle," she said giggling. "There were also those two bearded goats and the vodka cupcakes I made. I'm kind of a lightweight, regardless of what my hips say."

My eyes traveled to her tantalizing hips in her tight jean shorts, and I immediately regretted it. I could feel myself growing hard, and since I was wearing a wetsuit under my clothes, a hard-on wasn't something that could stick around.

"I would tell you what your hips say to me, but I'm pretty sure you'd slap me. I do have a surprise for you, and when we're done, we can share that bottle of wine. You shouldn't drink it alone. You might not make it home."

"Keep your *surprise* in your pants, Brady," she said, using air quotes with one hand while grasping the bottle tightly to her chest, "and I'm not sharing my wine."

Stopping in front of the shore of Lake Pendle, I tugged the bottle of wine from her grasp. It wasn't a struggle, but she almost tipped over trying to hold onto it. "The surprise isn't in my pants, though, you'd probably like that if you gave it half a chance."

"Probably," she said, that giggle filling the air again. A part of me wished I was recording her right now so I could prove to sober Haylee that drunk Haylee thought my manhood was worth taking half a chance on.

"Sit here," I said, directing her to an empty patch of sand amidst all the other onlookers. "The surprise will be out there," I explained, pointing to the water. "I'll be back in an hour."

"Give me back my wine," she slurred, her arms wrapped around her knees.

"I will...when I come back in an hour. I want to make sure you're still here when I get back. This," I said, holding up the bottle, "will ensure that you are."

The huffing sound she made was loud enough for everyone on the beach to hear. "I can't believe you're holding my wine hostage."

More like I was helping her sober up before she started drinking again. She'd thank me early tomorrow morning when she got up to bake without a raging hangover. "Not hostage," I insisted, holding it to my chest. "I just don't want you to drink it all without me."

"I have to get to the bakery and bake," she mumbled, struggling to stand but wobbling more than anything before she fell to her knees.

"God, no," I exclaimed, grasping her upper arm and helping her sit on her butt again. "Promise me you won't go to the bakery. That's a dangerous place to be in your condition."

Haylee tossed up a hand and let it drop to the sand. "I can't go anywhere. I forgot my keys and anyway, you have my wine. I'm forced to sit here and watch your *surprise*," she yelled, throwing those air quotes around again.

People were looking at us, but I didn't care. I was having too much fun with drunk Haylee.

"Remember, eyes out there," I said, pointing her head forward.

She started ooh and ahhing over the gorgeous blue water that she'd seen her entire life. Happy she'd forgotten about the wine long enough for me to escape, I darted over to the dock. After I stripped off my shirt and wrapped it around the wine, I tucked it away and strapped on a vest.

"Did you get lost?" the team captain asked when I was ready to go. "We've been waiting for you."

"Sorry," I said, even though I wasn't. "I had to help a friend. I'm ready. Let's do this."

Cupcake

The motor started, the crowd let out a ferocious roar, and I primed myself for the best sixty minutes of my week. At least it used to be the best sixty minutes of my week. Suddenly, the idea of sharing a bottle of wine with my cupcake filled that slot.

My cupcake?

Oh, boy.

What a show-off. There he was up there on top of that pyramid of water skiers like he was God's gift to women. Okay, so maybe he was, but still, it was annoying. I brushed some sand off my thighs and tried to avoid watching the waterski show out on the lake. Unfortunately, my damn disobedient eyes kept going back to Brady in that ridiculously tight wetsuit. Was it even a wetsuit? It was more like a leotard that was waterproof.

My loud, drunken laughter had people turning their heads to look at me, but I didn't care. The thought of Brady Pearson in a leotard was worthy of a few looks. His loaf of bread was prominent in it, and I was getting a little hot under the collar watching him up there, even from this distance. What must that be like up close and personal, I wondered. I shook my head and contemplated how he was going to get down from there. Wait. I peered closer with my hand to my eyes. Is he holding a flag with a strawberry on it?

I fell over onto the sand, laughing silently, my body shaking at the idea that the hot, ripped guy who's always taking up all the space in my bakery was wearing a skimpy wetsuit and flying around the water holding a flag with a strawberry on it. Sure, it took a massive amount of skill and muscles to pull off a pyramid on water skis without falling on your face, but a strawberry flag?

I grasped the paper program someone had given me at the start of the show and read the fine print. *Sponsored by the Lake Pendle Strawberry Festival.* Okay, now it made more sense. I grasped my knees to my chest and focused on the rest of the show. Brady did a backflip off the shoulders of the two guys he was on and landed in the water, waving to the crowd who all stood and cheered, yelling his name like he was Prince.

I glanced around embarrassedly when I realized I was also standing and yelling his name ridiculously loud. So much for playing it cool and not liking his surprise. I better find my poker face before he swims ashore and notices me ogling his hot body in his fancy suit.

While everyone else wandered away with their towels and beach chairs under their arms, I sat back down on the sand. I watched the sunset in the late evening breeze and waited for my bottle of wi—Brady. Sure, I had to work in a few hours, but if I stayed drunk the whole time, I wouldn't even care that I didn't get any sleep. The sun had set significantly lower in the sky by the time Brady showed up with his hair wet and a bag thrown over his shoulder. Unfortunately, it looked like his skimpy suit was no longer on his body. That was a disappointment.

"Hey there, cupcake. You're still here."

I stood and brushed the wet sand off my ass. "Of course. You took my wine. I would have appreciated you spending less time with your adoring fans, though. I'm thirsty."

All he did was smile, and that annoyed the crap out of me even more than usual. "It's a tradition that we talk to kids who are interested in potentially joining the team. It's called community service and recruitment. You should try it sometime."

"My life is community service and recruitment," I insisted, walking beside him. "I depend on the community to buy my cupcakes, so I recruit the very best ingredients."

Brady shoulder bumped me as we walked, and I nearly fell over. "Girl, you're still drunk."

"I don't remember the last time I was this drunk. For a little while, there were two of you on that pyramid. Color me surprised when I realized it was you out there doing all those fancy swirls and twirls in a skimpy leotard."

Brady's laughter could be heard the full length of Main Street. "It's called a wetsuit."

"I call it a tight suit. I'm not complaining," I said, holding my hands out in front of me and waving them around. "Your loaf of bread was definitely the highlight of the show." I slapped my hand over my mouth. "I mean, it was a great show."

"I'm glad you enjoyed it," Brady said, laughter in his voice. "I'm surprised you've never seen the show before. We perform twice a month during the summer and at every Strawberry Festival."

"I don't go to the beach much," I said with a shrug. "Besides, I'm usually sleeping by the time the show starts. I have a business to run. I can't be out gallivanting around all night like some people."

"It's barely nine p.m.," he answered, laughter coating the words. "Why are you out gallivanting around tonight, anyway?"

"You!" I said, tossing my hand up. "And where's my wine."

"In my bag. I thought it would be smart if you were home before you started drinking again."

"Shows what you know. Hand it over."

"What are you going to do? Swig it straight from the bottle?" he asked with one brow in the air.

"Absolutely." I made the gimme fingers until he pulled it from his bag and handed it over.

"Fine, but you might get a reputation if people see you staggering down Main Street drinking from a bottle."

"Can't be any worse than the reputation I already got," I muttered, my words still slurring. I brought the bottle to my lips and took a long pull of it, handing it back to him and wiping my lips on my arm. "Ahh."

"What the hell. If you can't beat 'em, join 'em." He slugged back a hit of the wine, and the sweetness made him cough and choke until he got his breath back.

I grabbed the bottle from him. "Can't hold your liquor, Pearson?"

"That's the girliest thing I've ever tasted in my entire life, and I work in a place that makes cupcakes."

I drank from it longer this time, smacking my lips when I finished. "All the more for me," I slurred, my steps uneven and crisscrossed.

"Somebody has to be sober in a few hours when it's time to start baking, and it sure as hell isn't going to be you," Brady muttered, taking my elbow to help me walk in a straight line.

He dutifully helped me up the stairs to my apartment, took the key, unlocked the door, and helped me to the couch. I fell hard onto the cushion and brought the bottle to my lips again.

"I'll be fine at four a.m. Unlike some people, I'm not a pansy-ass who can't work with a hangover."

"I can work with a hangover," he insisted. "I just prefer not to. Sit. I'll be right back."

"You're not the boss of me!" I yelled. "I'm your boss, remember?"

"Only when we're downstairs. Up here, I can boss you around, too."

"I don't think that's how this works!"

I grinned, enjoying this new side of Haylee. She was all kinds of funny drunk, which told me she would be funny sober, too, if she'd let her guard down. I bet Amber got to see her humorous side all the time. I was a little bit jealous that I didn't.

While she was busy swigging her sweet wine, I wandered through her tiny kitchen and finally found a frozen pizza in the freezer. I put it in the oven to bake and noticed the calendar on the side of the fridge. The page for July was missing, unless I slept through the whole month, but I didn't think so. When the coffee machine finished spitting out a cup of liquid gold, I carried it back into the living room, swapping the bottle of wine for the cup of coffee.

"I think you should ask for a refund on your calendar. It's missing the month of July," I pointed out, setting the bottle of wine out of sight.

"That's because Amber ripped it up. She said I had to stop focusing on my birthday," Haylee explained as she dutifully sipped the coffee. "She's a real buzzkill to a girl's goals in life. You know what? You're a real buzzkill with this coffee bit, too. If Amber were here, she'd let me have the wine."

"I've decided that Amber isn't always the best influence."

"Duh," she said, her eyes rolling around in her head, and she had to work hard to make them stop. "We've been friends since we were four. That was the day she convinced me that old Mrs. Daniels wouldn't care if we picked her flowers to give to Amber's mom."

"She cared?" I asked, laughter in my voice.

"Oh, she cared. Amber and I have been thick as thieves ever since."

The timer went off on the oven, and I stood, pointing at her. "Stay put and finish the coffee."

"Stay put and finish the coffee," she mimicked. "You're still not the boss of me."

Some men might feel emasculated with the constant reminders that she was the boss, but I wasn't one of those men. I preferred working for a woman. They most often were more willing to stop and think about other's suggestions before insisting something be done their way.

At least in my experience. Besides, Haylee was a lot easier on the eyes than my last boss, who had been six feet and nearly three hundred pounds.

After I stowed the rest of the wine in the fridge, I strode back into the living room, carrying the pizza and two plates. "Ta-da!"

Haylee lifted a brow at me and then started to clap slowly. "Wow. The baker managed to bake a frozen pizza." She pushed herself up off the couch. "Standing ovation."

I laughed and shoved her in the shoulder gently until she plopped back down on the couch. "Smart ass. Here, eat some of this now. Maybe you'll be sober enough by four a.m. not to burn down the bakery."

She bit into the pizza and moaned low in her throat. The sound made my dick jump in my pants on its own accord. All I could think about was that sound in my ear while I was bringing her to climax. The thought made me choke, and I coughed, covering it with a smile when she glanced at me sharply.

"You okay, bro?" she asked, taking another bite.

I swear she could see right through me and knew exactly what I was thinking. "Fine, thanks. I'm hungry, and it was too hot."

"I bet you worked up quite an appetite out there preening for the ladies," Haylee agreed.

"Waterskiing is hard work. It requires a lot of stamina. You should try it."

"Never going to happen," she said around the pizza in her mouth. "I can't swim."

"You can't swim?"

She shook her head until she swallowed the bite of pizza. "Not well. I'm all hips and ass. It's not pretty."

I so badly wanted to say it was pretty. So pretty. I knew better.

She had a second piece in her hand when I glanced up again. She held up the pizza. "See, this is the reason I'm all hips and ass. Pizza and cupcakes."

"You seem to think that being all hips and ass is a bad thing. At least that's the impression I've garnered over the last seven years."

The eye roll she gave me was powerful, and I would give it an eight out of ten if I were passing out scores. At least this time, she was able to bring them back to the center without as much effort. "As if you think being all hips and ass isn't a bad thing. Give me a break. I have a bridge for sale if you don't. Look at you with all your muscles in all the right places 'n shit."

I had to bite back my laughter, so I didn't choke on my pizza. "'N shit? I worked hard for these muscles just like you've worked hard on those hips and ass."

The pizza fell back to the plate, and the death glare she threw at me burned me to ash in the chair. "I've looked like this since the day I came out of the womb. Sometimes you're the ass."

"Why do you fight it then?"

"Fight what?"

"Being all hips and ass, to use your phrasing."

The pizza went back to her lips, and she took a bite, silently chewing while she glared at me. "Darla McFinkle."

"What about her?"

"She's the reason I fight it. Her, and Jerry, Tim, Tieg, and that asshole I had brunch with today. Matt? Mike? Moses? Max?" Her hand waved in the air. "Something like that."

"What about Darla? I'm confused."

"If you're confused, then you must be slow. Let me spell it out for you." Her hands made a stick straight figure to her left. "Darla McFinkle. Tiny and adorable since day one." She made a wavy line to her right. "Haylee Davis. A cupcake since day one."

I raised a brow. "A cupcake?"

"Look at me!" she said, bolting upright. "I look like a cupcake. Thick on the bottom, thin on top."

"Oh, I'm looking," I drawled appreciatively. "I look every day, but I'm smart enough not to take a bite." Her eyes rolled, and she sat again. "You're saying that Darla is the reason you hate on yourself all the time about your figure?"

"You would too after twenty-five years. Her nicknames weren't kind."

"Where do Jerry, Tim, Tieg, and today's asshole come in?"

She pointed at me while she chewed. When she finished that piece, she leaned back on the couch to relax. "They all spent a good portion of the date suggesting in not so subtle, and in a multitude of different ways, that my hips and ass were too big. The date I had today suggested I get a salad instead of a burger."

"Well, fuck them then. If you've been this way since the day you were born, what makes you think you can change it because someone points it out? Tell them to kiss your sweet ass and walk away. Why do you give them the power to make you feel bad about it?"

"I tried that once. It backfired on me, and now Darla knows she's got the power."

"I know I'm sober, but that made no sense, so it must be because you're drunk."

Her finger waved at me from across the room. "You asked why I named the bakery The Fluffy Cupcake?" I nodded and leaned forward, ready for the story. "Darla has called me a fluffy cupcake since the first day of kindergarten."

My finger went up in the air, and my mouth opened and closed a couple of times. It took me too long to come to a simple conclusion. "You named your business after the hateful nickname someone has called you your whole life?"

Her palm connected with her forehead, and she shook her head. "Dumb, I know. I thought I was thumbing my nose at Darla. Now she just gloats every time she struts in there like a queen. As if she got me, you know?" she asked, making the digging motion with her hand.

I shrugged and leaned back on the chair. "Only because you continue to let her think that."

Haylee swirled her finger around my face. "You've bought into this whole giving someone else the power thing, haven't you? Where the hell does that come from?"

"I had to learn early on that if I didn't have the power, I was the one who got hurt. You're living proof of that statement. I think you should own those hips and ass, and not just pretend to do it, either. You should own it and mean it every single time."

"Body positivity 'n shit?" she asked, a brow in the air.

"More like body acceptance. You need to start accepting yourself for who you are. The next time you date a guy who doesn't like it, tell him to kiss it and sashay those hips and ass right out of there. Next time Darla walks into the bakery, swing those bad boys out there, and hip-check her into next week."

"Accept me?" she asked as though she had to make sure she heard me right. "Like, all of me?"

My chuckle should have made her mad, but I think she was too curious to be mad. Apparently, the concept of accepting yourself was hard to grasp for drunk Haylee. "Yes, all of you. It's like you don't see that you're the owner of a wildly successful business that keeps half of this town fed every day, and provides all the memorable food for their special events. You don't see that you're the reason over half a dozen people are employed and making a living in a tiny town like this. Instead, you're always focused on what your hips and ass, your words not mine," I said, holding up my hands in defense, "look like in your work pants. At the risk of getting slapped or fired, I have zero problems with those hips and ass or the way they look in your work pants. I don't think being a fluffy cupcake is a bad thing. I'm not buying a bridge here, either. I've never been more serious about anything."

Her eyes widened, and she had to clear her throat before she spoke. "Oh, sure, because you've dated so many women like me, I'm sure."

"I haven't, but not for lack of trying. You're beautiful, and you deserve to be happy. Anyone who doesn't think so can fuck off."

"That's easy for you to say, Brady. You're a tall, strong, muscular guy that every woman wants to date."

My finger went up in the air again and paused. "Not every woman. There is one particularly stubborn one who won't date me. That said, the two of us," I whispered, motioning my finger between us, "we're not that different. We both came from places where we didn't get a lot of positive reinforcement about who we are as a person. If you think I don't know that you hired me because of my past, you don't give me much credit."

Her finger wagged back and forth as mine did. "That's not true. I hired you because you were qualified for the job, and I saw a hunger in you to find a community of people to call family. I once had the same hunger in me that I saw in your eyes that day."

My head nodded vigorously. "You just made my point. We're not that different."

Haylee stood and tipped to the right until I grabbed her shoulder and held her upright. "But we are. You're the guy every girl wants to land. I'm the girl every guy wants to pretend doesn't exist. At the very least, all they want to do is change me." Her hand waved dismissively in the air. "That's enough talking for one night. I'm tired, and you have to work tomorrow."

"Are you going to be okay alone up here tonight? Please, don't go down those stairs until you're steadier on your feet," I said, going to the door and grabbing the doorknob.

She crossed her heart and pointed down the hallway. "I'm going to fall into bed and sleep for about five hours. By the time I wake up, I'll be fine. Thanks for tonight," she said, waving and walking down the hallway, while I continued to stand by her door.

When she closed the bedroom door, I whispered the words that had been burning in my mouth since she spoke hers. "The very last thing I want to do is pretend you don't exist or change you, Haylee Davis. I would live the rest of my life happy to be wrapped around those hips and ass."

Ten

The air vents of the walk-in cooler blew a whisper of cold air across my neck. I might have noticed the shiver of charged electricity run down my spine if it weren't for the aggravation filling my soul. "Where are my eggs?"

Nothing annoyed me more than being told my station was ready for the day only to find a key ingredient missing. I was going to hunt him down, and—the eggs are still on the shelf!

"Gah! It must be Monday," I griped to the empty, cold space. I grabbed the tray and backed up to the door, nudging the handle with my generous bottom. It didn't budge. I pushed on it again, expecting the latch to click over, but it wasn't opening. "Great! Now I'm locked in the cooler!"

I absolutely did not need this today. I had a ton of orders to finish before we opened, and it was already five a.m. It didn't help that I had the slightest hangover from my excessive and embarrassing drinking escapades. I wanted to groan every time I thought about spending hours with Brady last night with my filter disabled. Drunk Haylee said things sober Haylee would never have said. Brady knew it, too. He took advantage of the situation. At least when it came to getting me to talk about the things I otherwise wouldn't talk about. Not going to lie, sober Haylee hates him a little bit because of it. Okay, she doesn't, but sober

79

Haylee *is* embarrassed and wishes she could do last night over.

I balanced the tray on one arm while I flicked the emergency button on with my free hand. That would shut down the cold air and alert those in the kitchen that I needed help. In the meantime, I had to cool my heels in here, quite literally.

"Did someone say locked in the cooler?"

Surprised by the intrusion, I spun around, jostling the eggs when the end of the tray clipped a shelf. Several smashed against my white uniform, leaving streaks of disgusting yellow goo dripping down my chest.

"Seriously, Brady!" I exclaimed, setting the remaining eggs down and searching for a towel.

He flicked his down off his shoulder and started swiping at my coat. "Sorry, I thought you knew I was in here."

I angrily snatched the towel away. I didn't like his hand so close to my chest or the way he caressed my breasts with every brush of the microfiber towel. Well, that wasn't entirely true. I liked it, but I would never let on. I thought about the conversation we'd had last night and decided I didn't need to egg him on. See what I did there? I snorted at my joke until his statement brought me back to the present.

"Why would I know that? You're always off doing something other than your job," I grumped. "I had no eggs at my workstation!" My hands flailed around while bits of eggshell floated through the air like confetti.

Brady shook his head with a sexy smile on his face. "You wear egg yolks surprisingly well, cupcake, but then again, you wear everything well."

He was not taking me seriously, and it was starting to piss me off. "The eggs, Brady. Why are they in here and not out there?" I asked, the volume of my voice increasing with each word.

When he grasped my wrist and lowered my arm, I couldn't help but notice his hand was still incredibly warm, even after standing in the cooler. I was starting to shiver, but if he kept touching me, I'd be hot and bothered in no time.

"The eggs are still in here because the recipe requires cold eggs. I couldn't put them out until you were ready for them. I guess you didn't read my note."

I tossed my hand up, the one he wasn't holding onto—still. "I didn't see a note! I have a ton of work to do, and now I'm stuck in here with you!"

His lid came down in a wink of sexiness that had me swallowing hard. "Anyone ever tell you that you're sexy as hell when you're all riled up."

"You're skating on razor-thin ice of sexual harassment, Brady," I said from between clenched teeth. Something in his smoldering expression of explosive maleness told me he didn't care.

He took a step closer to me until his white coat was sharing the splattering of yolks with mine. He pressed his hot, hard chest into mine and backed me up against the rack in the cooler. The contrast of temperatures was startling. The cold against my back grounded me while the heat of him against my breasts made them tingle with desire and anticipation. I hated and loved every single second of it.

"Really? Razor-thin?" he asked. I barely nodded and tried to swallow over the lump in my throat. "All I can say is, after seven years, it's sure as hell time to fall in."

His warm lips landed on mine, and in surprise, I grabbed the front of his coat and held on for dear life. His lips teased mine into not listening to me when I told them to stop kissing him. They kissed him back with everything they had, and the audible moan from my throat said I didn't even care. It said I liked the way the hard lines of his muscles pressed against me. It said I liked the way his hands kneaded my shoulders until his hand came up to grasp the back of my neck tenderly.

Unable to resist the temptation any longer, my traitorous hand slipped up to tangle in the soft hair at the nape of his neck. The silky-soft smoothness on my hand was a sharp contrast to his hard body and the way his lips were firmly planted on mine.

He angled his head in to get closer, to take the kiss deeper, his hand now pressed against my cheek to move my head to his desires. When the tip of his tongue ran along the ridge between my lips, another moan of desire ripped from my throat, right before my mouth fell open to allow his tongue entrance. Oh God, he was silky smooth everywhere.

He stroked my tongue with his in a way that said, ending up in his bed would never be a bad thing. When that magic tongue started its trek across the roof of my mouth, I nearly came right there surrounded by broken eggs and piles of cupcakes. Why did he have to be such a good kisser? This kiss was just going to make it harder to resist him. Everything was going to be awkward after—his tongue went back to mine to tangle with it roughly. It was almost as if he knew where my mind went, and he was going to drag it back one long stroke at a time. His hips bucked against mine, the hardness evident in his thin bakery pants proof of how affected he was by the kiss, too. He was most definitely enjoying this unexpected tangle of tongues.

Was it unexpected, though? He'd been trying to get in my pants for years, though I never believed it to be anything but a challenge he couldn't resist. A conquest he wanted to prove he could make. Now, I wasn't so sure.

His soft moan filled my head and drove every thought out of it, but how much I liked kissing him. It drove away every thought but how orgasmic it would be to make love to him with long, slow strokes until he came with my name on his lips. At the thought, my hips pressed into his, and my hand tightened against the back of his neck. I was desperate for air, but at the same time, I was desperate for the taste of him.

It was him who broke the kiss off abruptly, his chest heaving and his breath heavy on my lips when he rested his forehead on mine. "Tell me you felt that, Haylee. Tell me I'm not the only one feeling this way."

Cupcake

My head nodded, his bobbing with the motion. "I felt it. I don't think I liked it, but I felt it."

Brady's lips captured mine again for a too fast tumble until I was begging for air to soothe my burning lungs. I put my hand against his chest, and he reluctantly released my lips. "Still don't like it, cupcake?" he whispered, brushing a long piece of hair behind my ear.

I sagged against the rack and rested my forehead on his chest, so I didn't have to see his face and want to keep kissing his delectable lips. "We can't do this, Brady. We're not a good match. You're a playboy who isn't looking to do the same woman twice. I'm nearly thirty and looking to settle down. It won't work between us."

His hands grasped my ass and tugged me up flat against his hard, trim six-pack. The action allowed me to feel every inch of his loaf of bread, too, which was hard as steel. That was probably his plan. My hands wanted to know what it would feel like to hold him. Was he silky smooth there, too? Would he twitch in my hand when I ran my finger over his tip? The thought had me biting back a moan of needy desire. I was a hot mess, and I had to get away from him before I did something I shouldn't.

One hand still on my ass, he used his other hand to brush the hair off my forehead. "Cupcake, I'm nearly thirty-three, and there is only one woman I'm looking to do twice. I happen to be looking at her. I'm not a playboy, and I don't sleep with most of the women I take out, contrary to popular belief," he said, one brow raised in the air.

"Haylee?" Amber called from outside the cooler. "Are you okay?"

Brady was across the cooler mindlessly counting cupcakes by the time she yanked the door open two seconds later. "Oh, my gosh, were you guys locked in here?" she asked innocently.

Too innocently.

Damn this woman!

I grabbed what was left of my eggs and breezed past her. "We were, but everything's fine. Thanks for noticing the light." I lowered the eggs to the workbench and started cracking them into the bowl like I didn't just make out to the point of almost coming. Dammit! It had been too long since I'd had sex. That was the reason I was even considering what he said to be the truth. Did he mean I was the woman he wanted to do twice? I mean, he said he was looking at her, so he had to mean me, right?"

Amber brushed past me with a tray of cupcakes for the bakery case, a naughty grin on her face. I acted cool and calm while breaking my eggs into the bowl and waited for her to leave so I could freak out in private. "Did you get cold in the cooler?" she asked, her eyes drifting to my chest where my nipples peaked like Mount Kilimanjaro.

I crossed my arm over my chest, innocently. "It was pretty cold in there."

"Good thing you had Brady with you. His hotness surely kept you warm."

She sashayed into the other room with her cupcakes, and I groaned, my arm falling away from my chest. She didn't, did she? If she locked us in that cooler, I was going to have a word with her in private! What are you going to say? Are you going to thank her for giving you the best fifteen minutes of your life? The sound that left my throat was strangled, and I broke an egg too hard, the shells falling into the bowl with the yolk.

"I don't think the recipe calls for shells," Brady whispered from behind me, and I jumped, his nearness causing my dirty thoughts to flare back to life. "Let me help you with that," he whispered, his lips connecting with the back of my neck while he scooped the shells out with a spatula. "That's much better." He buried his nose in the back of my neck and inhaled deeply. "I hate and love how you always smell so good, cupcake. All I want to do is lick you...for starters."

I cleared my throat, his lips leaving trails of goosebumps down my back, and a shiver ran up my spine at the thought of him licking me. "I call it Eau de Cupcake."

He ran his thumb across the nape of my neck, and the sound he made could have been bottled and sold for sexual pleasure. "Mmmm, well, I'd eat your cupcake, cupcake."

He drifted off to his end of the workbench and began punching down loaves of bread, his breath heavy with every punch of the dough. If I didn't know better, I'd think he was frustrated. Then again, if he was feeling the same way I was, frustrated was too mild of a word.

Eleven

The bakery was finally closed, and I lowered myself to a chair at a table by the window.

"Tired?" a voice asked, and I raised my head to see Amber standing by the table, holding a sandwich and a cup of coffee.

I sat up and accepted the food and drink, offering her a smile while I took a bite. "Exhausted, but I think all the cakes are baked and ready for the morning. It's been a long day."

"Made longer by your need to walk around the other side of the bench rather than pass by Brady."

I moaned and dropped the sandwich back to the plate, resting my forehead on my palm. "He kissed me," I whispered, my voice barely audible in the now quiet building.

"Come again?"

I hadn't, but I still wish I had. That was the problem.

"Did you just say he kissed you?"

I nodded slowly without making eye contact. "When we were locked in the cooler." I lifted my head. "Wait a minute. How did we get locked in there if we were both inside, and you were the only other one here?"

She gave me the palms out. "Faulty latch?"

"Amber Phyllis Larson!"

"What?" she asked innocently. "It was an accident, I swear!"

"Accidently on purpose!"

She held up her hands. "It was an accident. I think I bumped into it when I got the first set of cupcakes out. I didn't realize it until I went back for more, which is the reason I then let you out."

"You didn't do it on purpose?" She swung her head back and forth, and I could tell she was being honest. "Well, regardless, it happened. Now I don't know what to do."

"About?"

I tossed my hands up in the air like a lunatic. "The kiss! Brady! Everything!"

Amber grasped my hand and squeezed it. "Talk to Amber about it, sweetie. What's the problem?"

I lowered a brow to my nose. "You know what the problem is. I'm his boss."

"Maybe, but that doesn't mean you don't need to get laid."

"Amber," I moaned, drawing out her name in frustration. "You know what I mean."

"Let's start at the beginning. Why did he kiss you in the cooler?"

"He smashed eggs against my coat by accident, and I got worked up."

"Shocker."

I lowered my other brow, and she snickered but stopped talking. "He said I was sexy when I was all riled up. I told him he was dangerously close to sexual harassment in the workplace, and he said then he might as well go all the way."

"But he didn't. Go all the way, that is."

"He went far enough! He kissed me, and—and grabbed my ass!"

She bit her lip, and whether it was to keep from being a smart ass, or to avoid laughing, I couldn't say. "I noticed he couldn't take his eyes off your ass all day. He even dropped an entire loaf of bread on the floor when he missed the pan."

"When I told him about the date last night with Maxwell, he told me I should own being all hips and ass.

He said he liked the way my hips and ass look in my bakery whites."

"And probably everything else, including those shorts you were wearing last night." I groaned, and her laughter rang out through the bakery. "I can't believe you kissed him."

I held up my finger. "Brady kissed me. I would never kiss an employee."

"But you kissed him back, right?"

I nodded and swallowed around the fear in my throat. "With tongue," I added, "but by not thinking, I put our whole business in jeopardy."

She held up her finger, pausing and licking her lips. "At the risk of sounding dumb, how did it put our business in jeopardy?"

"Duh, Amber! If he claims sexual harassment, we're done! We can't come back from that."

"Whoa, back up the bread wagon, Haylee. Brady kissed you, not the other way around. He also did it in a place where there were no witnesses. A sexual harassment claim would be he said-she said. He'd never win in court with that."

"He will in the court of public opinion. Who are they going to believe? The sexy guy or the thick chick? They're going to believe the sexy guy because why wouldn't a thick chick throw herself at a guy like him?"

Amber made the head explosion motion and shook her head. "You have serious self-confidence issues. I'm siding with Brady on that. Regardless, Brady isn't going to cry sexual harassment any more than you are. You're both adults, and you were both willing participants, right?"

"Seemed like it," I agreed. "He was moaning louder than I was. I broke off the kiss, and he dove back in for another until you interrupted."

"Dammit. I've always had bad timing!" she exclaimed, hitting herself in the forehead with her palm.

I chuckled and took another bite of the sandwich.

"That leads me to the next question," she said, and I motioned for her to ask it while I chewed. "Do you want to do it again?"

I moaned and closed my eyes. "So much, Amber. I'm trying not to think about the fact that I'll never do it again."

"Why the hell not?" she asked, her brow up in surprise.

I tossed my hand up and let it fall to the table, rattling the dishes. "Have you been listening?"

Her head nodded, but her smile was sneaky. "I heard you say he kissed you, you kissed him back, you both moaned, he liked it enough for a second kiss, and he loves your ass. All of those things seem like excellent reasons to do it again."

"Even though it could put our business in danger?"

Amber leaned back and crossed her arms over her chest. "It won't. Brady's not like that. He's also had the hots for you since he started working here. I'm not at all worried about it."

I stood up, my shoulders slumping. "I'm glad someone's not. Thanks for the food. You got the cleanup and lockup? I'm going upstairs to shower and try to forget about this day."

She stood and hugged me, how much she cared about me evident in her touch. "I've got this. Go rest up. Tomorrow is going to be just as busy. And stop worrying about this, please. I'd rather you spent some time thinking about the implications of kissing Brady in your personal life rather than your professional life."

I released her and headed for the back of the bakery. "That's the thing, Amber. The implications of Brady in my personal life are even scarier than the implications in my professional life. He could upset the bread cart here for a few months, but he could dismantle my personal life forever without even trying."

I took the steps to my apartment one at a time and hated how spot on those words sounded to my ears.

"Haylee, is that you?" Amber called out, and I frowned.

"No, it's Brady," I called back, walking into the front of the bakery. "I was looking for Haylee. I thought she'd be here."

Amber leaned on the counter and crossed her arms. "She left about twenty minutes ago. She was going home to shower and rest. Did you need something?"

I couldn't tell her that I'd come looking for Haylee to apologize for kissing her. Correction. Apologize for kissing her at work. I was struggling with the knowledge that if I did find my cupcake, I'd probably just kiss her again. I couldn't resist her now that I'd had a taste. Ever since I'd had her ass in my hands and my tongue in her mouth, I'd been walking around with half a hard-on. It was thoroughly uncomfortable. I needed more of Haylee Davis, and I wasn't going to pretend that I didn't.

"No, it can wait. I'll just talk to her about it tomorrow."

She shrugged and tipped her head to the side. "You could, or you could walk up the stairs and talk to her now. I know she wouldn't mind."

"It's not important enough to bother her with."

It was, but I would never tell my other boss that. Not when I'd made out with her best friend and business partner in the cooler when I was supposed to be working.

"I wish I could believe the words coming out of your mouth, but the look in your eye is a dead giveaway, Brady. If you think she didn't tell me about the kiss, then you don't know two women who are as close as sisters. We share everything. She's scared, and I'm not going to pretend that doesn't piss me off."

I held up my hands in front of me and took a step backward into the bakery. "I didn't do anything to scare Haylee. Don't be pissed at me."

Amber took a step forward and lowered a brow, her gaze raking me with an uncomfortable honesty I didn't like. "You didn't do it intentionally, but kissing her in the cooler produced the same result. Don't get me wrong. It was way past time the two of you stopped pussyfooting around each other and made out. The problem was where you chose to do it."

My hands fell to my side, and I nodded in agreement. "You're right, that's what I wanted to talk to her about." My hand went to my hair and lodged there while I searched for the right words to say. "She's scared because I kissed her in the cooler?"

"She's scared because you kissed her here, and that's a huge risk if you claim sexual harassment."

I couldn't stop the laughter that bubbled up from my chest. "Me? I'm going to claim sexual harassment."

Amber shrugged. "He said, she said. You won't win, but you can still do damage to this business."

"The business I'm a huge part of maintaining? The same business that has offered me new opportunities at every turn over the last seven years? That business?"

"I told her it was ridiculous, but you know Hay-Hay," she said on a shrug.

My head nodded before I thought about it. "I do. I also know it's a defense mechanism."

"Which she earned the right to have," Amber pointed out. "I'm sure you of all people understand that."

"While Haylee and I both grew up in the foster system, the difference is I had foster parents who loved me. Adoption wasn't a thing they did back then like it is now, and they were already old by the time I went to live with them, but they loved me like a son. They both passed shortly before I turned eighteen, but I knew they loved me. Haylee didn't have that."

"She lived with a lot of foster families around the area for the first ten years of her life. After that, she was placed with old Mrs. McNally. The social workers were always looking for a kid desperate enough for a stable place to live

91

that they were willing to be Cinderella and take care of Mrs. McNally."

"At ten," I said in disbelief.

"Hay-Hay did the work, and Mrs. McNally supplemented her social security. Not exactly win-win, but Haylee did have a place to live. My parents were her relief foster home, which meant she stayed with us one weekend a month. You know how that worked. It was supposed to be to give Mrs. McNally a break, but it was always to give Haylee one. We loved her, but it wasn't until my oldest sibling graduated when Hay-Hay was fifteen that we could take her in completely. It was a good thing because Mrs. McNally keeled over a month after Haylee moved out. She probably would have had to leave Lake Pendle if she couldn't live with us."

"I'm glad she has you and your family. Haylee's got grit, and while I know she comes by it naturally, someone still fostered the belief that she could be whatever she wanted to be. I have no doubt that was you."

"She has made something of herself despite the knocks against her," Amber agreed. "I don't want to see that ruined for her."

"That's why I came to apologize," I explained.

"You're going to apologize for kissing her?"

"Nope. I'm going to apologize for kissing her here, and then I'm going to kiss her again to prove to her I want to kiss her no matter where we are. Hopefully, I don't get slapped."

"Do we have a problem regarding the business, Brady?" Amber asked with one brow in the air.

I paused and thought out my answer. There was a right one and a wrong one, depending on what side of the bakery you were standing on. "The only problem we have regarding the business is how long it takes me to convince the other owner of it that I'm the guy she can trust to have her back—both in the bakery and her bed."

"That won't be easy. Hay-Hay doesn't let her guard down often."

92

The laughter that bubbled up inside me escaped at her words. "Do you think? I've been working here for a few weeks shy of seven years, and actively trying to get her to date me for six of those. The only reason I kissed her today was that the opportunity presented itself. If it hadn't, I'd still be wondering if she was ever going to notice me standing here day after day." My hand fell from my hair to my side with fatigue.

"Staring at her with so much devotion that's so obvious to the rest of us, you mean?" Amber finished, but I shook my head.

"Not devotion, no. Yes, devotion," I said on a sigh. "But not just devotion. Reverence, trust, belief in her and what she does for all of us. I don't know."

Amber pushed herself off the counter and walked toward me. "I think you do know. You know plenty. The person who doesn't know is upstairs. Even after you stuck your tongue down her throat with more passion than she's ever experienced, she still doesn't believe the hot guy wants to be with the thick chick."

The matching sigh we both let out was equally frustrated and sad. "Did Haylee say that? In that many words?"

"In those exact words. I've known Hay-Hay forever, and she hasn't changed since the day she moved into my family's home. She has always been the thick chick, and in my opinion, she's drop-dead gorgeous. If you think anything different, don't walk up those stairs. She's never going to look any different than she does today."

I strode to the back door and grasped the handle. "You're wrong, Amber. One day she will look different. One day, she'll look happy. One day, she'll look stunning in a white gown instead of white bakery pants. One day, she'll be glowing with the look of new life growing in her belly."

I swung out the door on the laughter of a woman I had hopefully just won over. I was going to need her in my corner.

One down. One to go.

Twelve

I sucked in a breath and stretched my neck out before I climbed the stairs to Haylee's apartment. I glanced down at the two boxes of food in my hands and prayed that she was still up. I planned to be here sooner but got caught up in the busyness of The Modern Goat. I had a couple of beers while I waited for the burgers, and suddenly, I regretted the mellow feeling they offered me. I had to be careful and consider this as important as anything I'd ever done in my life. No. This was the most important thing I'd ever done in my life.

At the top of the stairs, I knocked on the door and waited, bouncing slightly on my toes while I did so. I doubted Haylee was in bed already if she was as worked up about the kiss as I was, and I was still pretty damn worked up about it. Mostly because I wanted to do it again, all night and all over her.

"Coming," I heard her call out, and I groaned because the first thought I had was that I wanted to make her.

I noticed the door handle start to turn, but then it hesitated, likely because she was looking through the peephole to see it was me standing there.

"It's me, Haylee. I brought dinner."

"I was just going to bed, Brady," she said through the too-thin wooden door. I didn't like that anyone could break this door down in a matter of seconds. At least we lived in a town where the likelihood of that was slim.

"Please, Haylee?" I asked. "I just want to talk."

There was a beat of silence, and then the door swung open. "We don't have anything to talk about."

I walked through the open door and locked it behind me, setting the boxes of food down on the coffee table. "We do, but first, we eat."

She eyed the boxes from The Modern Goat. "Maybe I already ate."

"If you have, you can feel free to keep it until tomorrow, but something tells me you haven't because you're too worked up."

"Now you're a mind reader, too? Good to know."

I popped the boxes open and sat across from her, biting into a burger. "Nope."

She sighed with what could only be construed as frustration. Her eyes darted to the box of food. "Burgers and cheese curds. Looks like heaven."

I held up my burger. "It is. I know you gave Amber yours yesterday. Thought you might want a mulligan."

She shrugged before she disappeared into the kitchen, her tiny sleep shorts sending a zing of awareness straight to my groin. When she came back, she had a bottle of wine and two glasses. She poured us each a glass and then sat before she finally picked up her burger and took a bite. Her eyes rolled back in her head as she chewed. "I love their food. It's always so fresh."

"Including these thick, crusty rolls they use for buns. Wonder where they get them from?"

Her laughter filled my head, and my heart soared. That was precisely what I wanted. I wanted her to relax and enjoy a meal with me the way we used to. The way we did before the painful awareness of our mutual attraction stole that away. It had been years, but tonight was different. It felt to me like the kiss in the cooler took the edge off that electric charge zinging between us. Sure, it also supercharged it, but with that first kiss out of the way, we weren't left to wonder if kissing each other was what we wanted. It was. Now we just had to figure out where to go from here.

For now, we'd eat burgers and cheese curds and sip the wine she had disappeared into the kitchen to get before she started on her meal. That helped, too. She was extending an olive branch to me in her home. It wasn't about being a good hostess, though. It was about her knowing it would help us both with the conversation to come.

I leaned back on the couch and drank the wine while she finished her food. It was glorious to sit here and just observe her somewhere other than the bakery. Every inch of her ivory skin was glowing, and if I had to guess, also softer than a down pillow. I knew her ass was. When I had it in my hands earlier today, I was breathless. I had found heaven after six long years of searching, and I wanted to stay in that cooler forever. The memory alone made my dick harden without conscious thought. I wish she understood how incredible she was in all aspects of her life.

She didn't.

She didn't see that she could bake circles around me without even trying. She didn't see that she was more than Darla ever could be simply because she was kind. She didn't see that her beauty knocked the breath from me every time I saw her. One day she would. One day I would open her eyes and teach her to love the real Haylee Davis.

She leaned forward to grasp her wine glass, and her tiny sleep shorts pulled up another inch, leaving little to my imagination. I moaned and then cleared my throat, so I didn't choke on the wine. "I don't suppose I could convince you to cover yourself with a blanket?" I asked, my voice needy and thick with desire.

Her brow went up, and she tugged on her sleep shorts before she checked to make sure her tank top hadn't dipped too low in the front. It didn't matter. I could see the outline of her nipples through the fabric, and I wanted nothing more than to suck them between my lips and tease them until she came under me.

"What? Suddenly you can't stand to look at the hips and ass you said you didn't have a problem with just a day ago?"

She wanted the question to sound flippant and uncaring, but it didn't work. I heard the hurt that filled those words. I set my wine glass down and stood slowly, my khaki shorts unable to hide the truth when I was standing. "Does this look like I can't stand to look at them? No, just the opposite is true. I love looking at them, but if you don't cover up, I won't be able to form a coherent sentence in another two minutes."

She tugged a blanket off the back of the couch and covered her legs with it. Her nipples still begged for my touch, but I'd accept only suffering half as much pain right now. "Thanks for dinner. It was nice not to have to hear about how I should eat a salad when I really wanted a damn burger."

I sat again and tried to adjust my pants, so every movement didn't cause shooting spasms of desire through me. "You'll never hear that from my lips, Haylee. You're an adult, and you make your own decisions. Sure, in this case, I made the decision, but I didn't think you'd mind."

Her smile was genuine when she lowered her wine glass. "I didn't mind at all. I appreciate dinner. Sorry about being rude earlier. You took me by surprise."

I shook my head and leaned forward over my knees. "You weren't rude. You were cautious, and I get that. I showed up unannounced. I should have called or texted, but I was afraid you'd say no."

"Probably would have," she agreed, chuckling. "I'm glad you didn't call ahead. I would have missed out on that amazing hunk of meat and…you."

"Another amazing hunk of meat?" I asked, laughter in my voice.

"Some would say."

"What do you say, cupcake?"

"I say you should stop calling me cupcake, but you won't."

"You're excellent at diversion, do you know that?"

Her shoulder went up in a shrug while she tipped her wine glass up again. "I wanted to talk to you about something, Brady."

I held up my hand to stop her. "I know, that's why I'm—"

"No," she said with a head shake. "I'm first." I sighed internally but motioned for her to go ahead. "I made a mistake."

"I don't think so—" Her withering look had me stopping midsentence.

"As I was saying. I made a mistake when I offered you the position doing inventory for the bakery."

Was she fucking kidding me with this? I kiss her once, and she starts backtracking on all the progress we've made over the last seven years?

"I offered you the position because I was scared."

"Color me confused, Haylee. I thought you offered me the position because you trusted me to have your back in the bakery. I thought I'd finally proven myself as a team player in your business."

She refilled her glass, tossed it all back, and set the glass down, leaning forward to give me a shot down her shirt that only served to make my dick even harder. Forget a cold shower tonight. I was going to have to immerse myself in ice to forget about those creamy breasts that would overflow in my hands if I ever got the chance to hold them.

"You have proven yourself in the bakery, Brady. There's no question that you're a team player or that you have my back. If you weren't there every day doing what you do, I couldn't do what I do. I know that, so do you."

"What's the problem then?" I asked so confusedly I had to shake my head to clear it. Was the wine playing tricks on me here?

"The problem is the position I offered to you."

"The one you offered me because you were scared."

She leaned back and pointed at me, which took away the fantastic view of her tight nipples that were just waiting for my lips.

"Okay, so what do you want to do about it? You want to take over the ordering again?"

"No, we're going to do the ordering together, but Taylor will do the rest of the kitchen manager duties. She wants more hours, and Amber said she'd be fine with splitting her between the front and the back of the bakery."

I waved my hand around. "Wait, you're going to give me less responsibility because you're scared? That's kind of screwed up, Haylee."

She bit her lip, but I was the one who had to bite back a groan at the motion. She had no idea how sexy she was all the time. I wouldn't mind teaching her, but per the discussion we were currently having, that wasn't going to happen.

"I'm making a mess of this," she sighed, leaning forward to pour more wine, but I stopped her hand.

"Please, tell me what I'm supposed to do. I'm lost."

"I want you to work the bench with me full-time," she said in a rush, her breath warm on my arm.

I sat back in surprise, my brows up in the air. "You don't want me to be the kitchen manager at all?"

She swung her head wildly, and her curls bounced around her head. "You'll help me with the ordering of what you'll need as the master baker of breads and buns. I'll be the master baker of cakes and pastries. Taylor will take care of all the other kitchen manager duties."

"Master baker of breads and buns?" I repeated, and her head nodded hesitantly.

"If you want, that is. If you're happy doing what you're doing, I'll figure something else out."

"If I want to be promoted to a position that I've been working toward for years?" I asked slowly, and she nodded again. "I'm not a master baker, though."

"Yet," she answered. "I sent in the paperwork to prove your experience, and I know you've taken the written test. I assume you've passed it?"

"With flying colors," I agreed. "I took the practical test, too. I haven't heard if I passed yet."

"You did. I don't even have to think about it. You're a talented baker, Brady. Without you, The Fluffy Cupcake would still be making cupcakes and nothing else. It's because you were determined to expand the product line that we have as many standing orders for buns and bread as we do. A good portion of our income comes from those orders, too. I might be scared, but I'm also a businesswoman who can see that I need to use my talent wisely. I've been wasting it instead. That's over now."

I rubbed my forehead and peeked at her under my hand. "I'm still confused about the scared part. Were you scared I'd say no, or what?"

"No," she said, pouring another glass of wine and drinking it all before finishing her answer. "I was nervous about changing the dynamics in the bakery and how we get things done day-to-day."

"I'm there every day, cupcake. The only difference is, now I'll be at the bench and not in the back."

She tipped her wine glass at me and grimaced. "Exactly."

"That's what scared you," I said, not as a question but as a statement. "Working with me every day."

Her head bobbed in agreement. "That would be the reason. If you're at the bench all the time, I might," she paused and then just shook her head. "I don't know."

"I think you do. Tell me what you were going to say, Haylee."

She stared at me stubbornly, her eyes hooded and not meeting mine. "I was going to say that working with you at the bench all the time will make it hard to keep you at arm's length. You know how closely we'll be working together if we're both baking full-time. It's hard enough for me when you're in the back half the time."

"What's hard enough?" I asked, standing and moving over to sit by her. I had no sooner sat than she stood, walking to the opposite wall and leaning against it. Her damn tiny shorts were going to be the reason my shorts got wet in another few seconds.

Dammit. She was fucking exquisite.

Cupcake

I swallowed at the thought of running my hands down those hips and grabbing her ass. I wanted to hoist her legs around my waist so I could bury my hardness in her. I was aching to relieve the pressure that had been building inside me for years. Pressure I wasn't sure I would be able to contain working beside her day after day. I'd have to, though. The only thing I wanted as much as I wanted Haylee Davis was a full-time baking gig.

"Staying away from you," she finally answered. "Not touching you. Not wanting more from you than your talent with the dough. That will be hard and scary, but you deserve this. I can't pretend you don't. I know you could have gotten a job as a full-time baker anywhere else by now."

I stood and stalked toward her, stopping just short of plastering myself against her softness. My dick was hard, and I couldn't hide it. I didn't want to. Maybe seeing the proof of what she did to me would help her to believe my words. "I absolutely could have."

"Why did you stay at The Fluffy Cupcake all these years then?" she whispered, the question hesitant.

"Because of you, cupcake. There is no other bakery in the world that has anyone as gorgeous as you are working for them. I would mop the floor of The Fluffy Cupcake with a damn toothbrush if it meant I could keep seeing your sweetness every day. Career aspirations are one thing, but life goals are another. My life goal is to make Haylee Davis my cupcake. Full stop."

Thirteen

The air around me was electrified, and he was closing in on my space. Did he just say his life goal is to make me his cupcake? Um? My eyes traveled the length of him and paused at the outline in his pants that told me one part of him was dead serious.

"You—you don't mean that," I stuttered, my words slurring slightly from all the wine. "You just want to get in my pants. It's like a challenge for every guy to fuck the thick chick and then walk away, right?"

With his left hand on the wall next to my head, he rubbed the front of his shorts with the right. "Oh, I want to get in your pants, but I have no intention of walking away. I should have said I want Haylee Davis to be my cupcake for eternity."

"Eternity," I whispered.

He nodded that Adonis head at me.

"I originally came over here tonight to apologize for kissing you."

And there we have it. He already had regrets, and he hadn't even gotten in my pants. Thank God for that. "See, already wish you hadn't."

"Wrong," he said, leaning in closer now, both hands braced on the wall. "Wish I hadn't done it in the middle of the bakery? Yes. Wish I had waited until you didn't have to worry about me claiming sexual harassment? Yes. Wish I hadn't kissed you? Absofuckinglutely not. That was the hottest kiss I've ever shared with anyone, and we were in the middle of a damn cooler."

I swallowed around the lump in my throat. "You talked to Amber."

"I did, but I didn't need to do that to know I'd made a mistake. That's why I was back at the bakery after I showered. I wanted to tell you it wouldn't happen again—in the bakery, at least. I was going to kiss you when we were at the lake, and then the other night when we were here alone, but I chickened out."

"You chickened out?"

"Why do you keep repeating everything I say?" he asked teasingly.

"Because I'm having a hard time wrapping my mind around the idea that you wanted to kiss me, regardless of the place."

"Kiss every part of you until I can bury this deep inside you, you mean?" he asked, taking my hand and holding it against the front of his pants. "This is what your little shorts do to me. We aren't even going to talk about how much I want to pull one of those beautiful nipples between my lips and swirl my tongue around it." His hips thrust against my hand, and the air snapped and crackled like a summer storm over the lake.

"I—I don't know what to say," I stuttered without dropping my hand. He was hard, huge, and his dick jumped every time I caressed it. Brady didn't have an average *I want to get lucky hard-on*, either. This was the hard-on of a guy who had spent a lot of frustrating nights alone. He just wanted the woman he'd been dreaming about to finally open up to him, both her mind and her legs.

"Say you'll accept my apology so I can kiss you again. Here, where no one can misconstrue what is going on as anything but what it is."

"What is it?" I asked breathlessly while his lips traveled down the length of my neck to my collarbone.

"A man tired of waiting for a woman to realize she's the only one he's wanted for six long years, but respects that her place of business is not the place to show her that."

"I accept your apology," I moaned when he nipped at the skin near the edge of my tank top.

He growled somewhere low in his throat before he pinned me up against the wall with his hard body and buried both hands in my hair. When he tipped my head to the right, his hungry eyes filled with a fogged passion that could no longer be denied. His lips stole the breath from mine in a fierce pounce. Before I could suck in another breath, he pried my lips open and pushed his tongue inside to swirl through my mouth with the ferocity of a summer tornado. He was lit up with desire, and all I could do was hang on or risk getting sucked into the eye of the storm.

His hand slid from my hair and down to rest at my waist. The tremble of desire rocking his body told me how hard it was to hold back and keep his hand there. He wanted more, I could tell, and when I wrapped my arm around his neck, his hand slid down to cup my hip. His fingers kneaded it while his tongue kept my mind tied up in the sensation of velvet. When I moaned, his competing moan filled the room again, as though he was waiting for me to go first before he voiced his opinion.

He pressed me up against the wall with his body, his hardness twitching against my stomach, and both hands holding my ass like a prized possession. I swear he wanted to lift me up to wrap my legs around his waist, but I knew he wouldn't be able to hold me up for very long.

"Fuck, Haylee," he hissed, taking his lips off mine for a second to breathe. "How can you even question how incredible you are? A few more minutes of this and I'm going to come like a teenage boy. I almost welcome it if I'm honest. It's physically painful to be this hard and never get any relief."

"There are ways," I said, my brow up in the air as he held his forehead to mine. "There are things you can do to relieve the pain."

His hips thrust against my stomach again, and he moaned in a way that made me seriously worry he was going to come like a teenage boy. "I know the ways. I use the ways frequently after spending eight hours a day with you wearing those tight bakery pants over this sweet ass," he said, his hands caressing it again. "But the pain remains. Making myself come relieves the physical pressure, but it doesn't relieve the emotional need to be with the person you desire the most." His sharp intake of breath made my nipples go hard under my shirt. "I can't believe I'm holding you up against the wall telling you how much I'd rather fuck you than masturbate."

I couldn't decide if the moan that filled my head was mine or his. I wasn't sure it mattered. We both wanted the same thing. I had to decide if I was willing. I had no doubt he was. His lips were back on mine in a hungry dance of lust, longing, and six years of pent up sexual frustration. A girl can have her cake and eat it, too, right?

"Would it help if I told you that when I come alone, your name is on my lips?" I asked.

His dick jumped against my hand again at my words, and his growling moan filled my head when he nipped at my collarbone like a starved man. Before I could react, his tongue trailed along the edge of my breast to dip into my cleavage.

"That doesn't help. Now I'm just picturing that in my mind. Please don't tell me about all the other guys you've been with lately. I will get possessive."

Laughter lifted my chest until his nose was buried between my breasts. "I haven't been with a guy in years, Brady. I don't sleep around, and as I learned this past year, it's challenging to find a guy who's interested in these hips and this ass."

His teeth nipped my breast and drew a sharp hiss from my lips. "It wasn't that challenging, baby. I was standing right there, but you were too blind to see it. Do you finally see it?" he asked, tugging me toward him by my ass.

"I feel this," I said, caressing his dick with my knuckles. "I don't understand it, but I feel it."

He pressed his full weight into me until I was up against the wall again. His nose was buried in my neck, and his breathing was ragged. "What's to understand? Everything about you is a fucking turn on, cupcake. From your brain to your beauty, to your—"

"Brawn?" I asked sarcastically, seeing where it was going.

"No, to your baking skills and business acumen. I can bake, but you create. I have learned so much working for you, and that's the only reason I passed the master baker test. We both know it. All of you, every part from your inability to see how fucking sexy you are, to the self-conscious way you try to hide this ass under a chef coat that is way too big, to the way you pretend like you don't want to fuck me, is a turn on."

"Maybe I don't want to fuck you," I said haughtily.

His lips were on mine before I finished the words, and his tongue thrust in and out of my mouth, giving me an ample idea of what he wanted to do with his steel hard-on.

"Your lips tell me otherwise," he said, lifting his off mine to speak. "Your lips, and these gorgeous nipples," he said, strumming one with his thumb, "tell me you want me to take you down to your bedroom, spread you out on that bed, grab this ass and bury myself inside you until we both find the completion we didn't have until we found each other."

"Your self-confidence is astounding," I teased, bracing my hand on his chest, so I didn't grasp ahold of his dick and start caressing him again. That was something I could get used to, and I most definitely should not get used to caressing him.

"And yours is absent," he whispered, his brow raised for a moment until he dipped his head down for a kiss to my lips. "I'm going to find it and bring it back."

"Self-confidence has to come from within, Brady," I reminded him, even if my voice was breathy.

"You will be coming from within, Haylee. And when you're done, and those muscles relax, you'll notice your self-confidence has fought its way back to the surface."

Cupcake

"You really think taking a ride on your pole is going to do all that?"

"No," he said, shaking his head, his hand caressing my cheek. "The way I make love to you will do that. The slow, torturous way I'll strip your clothes off. The way your nipple will beg for me to keep suckling it, even as your thighs part for my fingers. The slickness I'll discover there will make me moan at the thought of how good it will feel to sink inside you and finally rest for the first time in six years. When I come with your name on my lips, without another thought other than how good it feels to have you come around me, you'll start to understand how I will never be full of your cupcake. That's what will bring that self-confidence out for the first time since I've met you."

I rested my forehead on his chest and took a shuddering breath. "If we do that, Brady, everything changes. How do we work together again? How do I manage you as your boss when you've tasted my cupcake in that way?"

He wrapped his arms around me and massaged my ass with his magic fingers. "The same way you did today and all the days before that. I can fuck you at night, and still take direction from you during the day. I'm not a twenty-year-old kid who can't separate the two. The Fluffy Cupcake is your business, and I'm just grateful that I get to keep working there with you. My manhood does not ride on the idea that I can't or won't take direction from a woman. Never has, never will. My manhood rides on the idea that I can take direction from a woman during the day and fuck her senseless every night without conflict ruining that arrangement. I'd rather that was what represented my manhood than beating my chest like an animal while claiming I had the biggest dick in the room."

"In this case, you do," I said, taking a full tour of him again. He was long, so very long, hard, and pulsing. There was a small spot of wetness on his shorts that left no doubt as to his desires.

"In this room, yes, I have the biggest dick, and I know how to use it. In the room downstairs, you have the biggest dick, and honestly, that turns me the fuck on more than anything else. You don't mess with Haylee Davis. I learned early on that paying attention to what she had to say and what she could teach you were what showed your intelligence, not trying to one-up her skill with skills you don't have yet."

I stared up at his face, my hand coming up to caress the stubble at his cheekbone. "You make yourself out to be untalented and uneducated. That's so far from the truth. You're incredibly skilled at what you do, Brady. I've learned just as much from watching you work with bread dough as you have from me with everything else."

"That's what makes us the perfect team. That's also why I'm not worried that after I make you come multiple times tonight, we won't be able to walk downstairs in the morning and keep doing what we've always done."

I grasped his hand and walked backward toward the bedroom.

"Where are we going?" he asked, his feet following me reluctantly.

"To my bedroom. You said you wanted to see my cupcake. Did you change your mind?"

"Hell no," he answered, his hand back on my ass, kneading, caressing, and moaning at the feel of it under his hand. "I can't wait to get this ass bare." He groaned then, and it wasn't a sound of pleasure. I swung my head back to stare at him with a question in my eye. "I don't have any protection," he said. "Dammit. Is the pharmacy still open?"

I turned and braced my hands on his chest. "I'm afraid not."

"Then we can't go that far, but we will take care of business to get us through until tomorrow night."

"I haven't been with anyone for years, but I'm still on the pill, Brady. What about you? I know you have dated a lot."

He grasped my chin and kissed my lips hard, nipping, and biting at them until our chests were heaving. "Dating a lot and sticking Little Brady in everything that walks are two different things, Haylee. I don't. The women I have been with have been few and far between, and I always wore a condom. I think the last one was about three and a half years ago."

"Wait. What?" I asked, my head tipped to the right. "I know you've dated women since then."

His finger trailed down my cheek as he backed me up toward the bedroom door. "I have, but I didn't sleep with them. There is only one woman who makes my dick this hard. I'm looking at her. I kept trying to find a woman who made me as hard as you do with just a look, but there were none."

"No wonder you're in pain then," I said, a frown on my face. "Three years is a long time to be celibate. Were you ever going to tell me?"

"Why do you think I kissed you in the damn cooler today? I couldn't take the pressure of waiting for you to notice me any longer. You've rebuffed my advances for years. I knew you were scared then, and I know you're scared now. I also know we can't keep pretending we don't want this, can we?"

My head swung mutely, and he grasped my cheek, holding it still. "It would be kind of hard now," I agreed.

"It's definitely hard. Harder than it has ever been," he teased.

"I think I know how to relieve that." I sat down on the bed and tugged him between my legs. "It starts by removing these." I unhooked his belt and lowered his zipper, but his hand grasped mine before I got any further.

"Not so fast, cupcake. I've dreamed about this for six years. I'm calling the shots."

"Where does this little fantasy begin?" I asked, leaning back on my palms.

"With you wearing fewer clothes. Let's start there."

He stripped my tank top over my head to reveal my plump breasts. "Fuck, cupcake," he said, his eyes pinned to my chest. My eyes were pinned to his dick bobbing in his pants in reaction to them.

"Lie back, gorgeous."

I did what he asked, my legs still hanging off the bed when he knelt on it, his eyes traveling the full length of my chest before his finger trailed down my right breast. "My mouth is watering," he whispered before his lips captured the left nipple in his teeth. While his tongue teased that one into a peak, his hand massaged the other one, his moan humming through my chest.

"Better than the dream?" I asked, the last word ending in a moan when he switched breasts to lick and suck the other one.

"Hell yes," he moaned, kissing his way down my bare belly to my navel. His tongue dipped in, making me buck with pleasure. It was when my ass hit the bed again that I registered my sleep shorts were gone, and I was bare to him.

His hand went to the front of his shorts to stroke himself while he stared at me wide open to his gaze. I tried to cover myself with my hand, but he grasped it.

"Don't you dare think about covering up this kind of mouthwatering cupcake."

"You can look, but you can't touch. Not when you're wearing that many clothes."

"What about eating that cupcake? Is that allowed?" he asked, stripping his shirt off to reveal a chiseled chest covered in fine, barely-there blond hair.

I chuckled, a smile lifting my lips seductively. "You want to eat my cupcake?"

His moan filled the room for seconds before he could speak again. "First, I want to lick it. Then, once I've had a taste, I'm going to nibble at it so I can savor the experience. Then I'm going to dip my tongue in to taste the sweetness waiting for me before I gobble it up until your cupcake is nothing but crumbs on my tongue."

"Fuck, Brady," I hissed, my earlier modesty gone and my hips thrusting into the air.

"That's what I'm going to do when I finish eating."

"If you'd take those pants off, I could knead your bread while you snack on my cupcake."

Cupcake

His growl was accompanied by the flinging of his shorts across the room. When his bread bounced free, it was my moan that filled the space. "Brady," I sighed, my hand caressing his velvety skin. "This is the most magnificent loaf of bread I've ever seen. God, I want to taste you so much right now." My thumb swiped its way through the moisture at his tip, and I sucked my thumb off while gazing up at him. His eyes had gone black with desire, and he pushed me backward gently, kneeling and lifting my legs over his shoulders.

"You're the magnificent one. Now, let me have my snack."

He kissed his way up each thigh, stopping just short of my cupcake each time to tease me. When he did what he promised and took a lick, I cried out. My thighs quivered with desire until he parted them further. His nose nuzzled into the crevice of my center to kiss along each lip before he licked the full length of me. Another moan ripped from my lips, and I crushed my thighs against his ears.

"You promised we could both have a snack," I said, my greediness to taste him the way he tasted me too much to fight.

"I don't know, baby. I'm pretty happy where I am," he said against the center of me, making my hips thrust upward to get closer to his tongue.

"I could make you happier," I said on a sigh.

"I'm a smart enough man to know that's true," he agreed, lowering my legs to the floor.

I scooted backward, and he situated himself, motioning for me to throw a leg over his chest and back up to his lips.

"I'll crush you," I said awkwardly, but he grasped my leg rather than answer, leaving me no choice but to swing it over him.

"Holy hell, cupcake. This ass is going to be the death of me," he hissed right before his hands grasped it, and his tongue went back to the snack he'd been enjoying.

He was hard and bobbing with desire, and the moisture waiting at his tip was more than I could resist. My tongue darted out and captured it, sucking gently to taste his saltiness. His hips bucked, and I swallowed him deeper than I'd planned, holding him there while his moan rocketed through the both of us at lightning speed. I sucked him in deeply twice, enjoying the shiver that ripped through him each time. When I let him slip from between my lips, I licked him up and down while he hummed with desire against my thighs. On a breath, I sucked him in deep again and moaned with him for a long thrust. It was my turn to laugh against his tip when his thighs shook uncontrollably. I was ready to gloat until he slid a finger inside my wetness to tease me while his tongue licked and sucked.

"Oh, you're as sweet and wet as I knew you'd be," he hissed, his hot breath blowing on my core until I shivered. "As much as I love having my dick in your mouth, I want to be in this sweet cupcake even more."

He deftly flipped me over until I was under him, and he was kneeling over me like a hawk, his lips on mine again in a hungry tangle of tongues. I was so turned on I was worried the bed was going to combust soon if we didn't blow off some of this steam. "I still don't have any protection. You're okay with that?"

"I didn't think you'd knitted any while you were busy eating your snack," I said, against his lips. "I want to feel your warmth inside me, Brady," I whispered, grasping his face in my hands. "I want you to fill me with your need and desire. All of it, every last drop."

"I don't deserve you, cupcake," he hissed, his hands already gripping my hips to pull me toward the end of the bed. "I sure as hell am going to oblige you, though. Wrap your legs around my waist," he ordered. Once I did, he grasped my ass and held me up in the air. "If I have you once, I'll never get enough. Do you understand me?"

My head nodded before I thought about it, and he plunged inside me with a ferocity I wasn't expecting but welcomed all the same. Our moans mingled when he buried himself all the way to my core and paused, waiting for me to relax. "God, Brady," I cried, the room hazy around me as I focused on him and nothing else. "It's never been like this before." His hands lifted my hips, and he sank into me another inch, all of him surrounded by my wetness.

"For me either," he growled, his hands stroking my hips while he stayed buried deep inside me without moving. "I don't want to move and end this feeling."

"If you don't move, I can't make you feel even better."

His hips bucked then, and I locked my ankles behind him, thrusting him back inside me. His hands used my hips as handles while he pumped in and out of me slowly, drawing me up to the clouds but not letting me stay there. Every moan, every thrust, every time he breathed my name in that voice of disbelief and reverence, I wanted to come around him. I was filled with an emotion I couldn't name, or maybe I just didn't want to.

He leaned down, capturing my lips and thrusting his tongue into my mouth in the same rhythm he thrust his hips. "Fuck, Haylee," he moaned, his hips thrust deep and still. "I'm so close. I don't know if I can hold back much longer."

I grasped his face, holding him close to my lips. "Don't hold back. I'm so ready to fly with you, please."

His hips thrust forward again, and his lips were on mine before my words died off. He broke off the kiss, lifted my ass with his hands and pumped into me, pressing his thumb to my swollen, engorged button until I moaned, the waves of release starting at the same time I called his name. "Come with me, Brady!" I called, my voice distant to my ears.

"You're ruining me, cupcake," he answered, buried deeply inside me as I spasmed around him. "Oh God," he called, and then his warmth filled me as I milked every last drop of emotion from him until he collapsed against me, his nose buried in my neck as we searched for air in a room that was filled with nothing but emotion.

He pressed his groin into me, and let the shudders rack him with every breath.

"I wasn't expecting that," I admitted, rubbing his back once we caught our breath.

"I was," he whispered, his breath tickling my neck. "I was."

I waited, but he said nothing more.

Fourteen

The door to the cooler opened and then closed again in quick succession. I glanced up, startled from my daydreams of Brady cupping my cupcake, to see my bestie standing by the cooler door, holding the handle closed.

"What's up?" I asked, going back to my cupcake counting.

"What's up? I don't know, but something is!" she hissed, her cheeks red and her eyes wild. "We aren't leaving here until you tell me what it is!"

I pushed the tray of black forest cupcakes back onto the rack and stifled a yawn. I didn't get more than thirty minutes of sleep between rounds of making love with Brady last night. Wait. Can I call it making love? It was just sex, right? Lots and lots of sex. I sighed internally. I'd been having this argument with myself all morning, and I was getting nowhere fast.

"I don't know what you're talking about, Amber. Nothing is up. Are you okay?"

Amber huffed and tossed her hand onto her hip. "It's almost nine a.m., and you two are standing out there with the most ridiculous grins on your face that I've ever seen! Something is up! I know he came to your apartment last night to apologize for the kiss."

"Oh, he came," I agreed, biting my cheek to keep from grinning to hard. "Many times."

115

"Shut up!" she exclaimed, falling to one knee. "Shut up, shut up, shut up!"

I stared at her silently until she motioned for me to speak. "You just told me to shut up four times."

"Talk," she hissed, "it's cold in here."

"Long story short, he brought dinner, we ate, I talked to him about taking over as full-time bread baker, and then things devolved to no underwear and lots of sex."

"Haylee! What the hell? With Brady? Finally?"

There was so much shock, surprise, awe, confusion, and questions inside her that I didn't know what to address first.

"Yes, with Brady. I'm not sure about the finally part."

Her eyes rolled nearly all the way around before she pinned them on me again. "Pretend all you want, but we both know finally is the perfect word. You've been dancing around each other for years! Oh my God!" she exclaimed, waving her hand in front of her face. "I think I'm having a heart attack. I need to sit down."

"Don't be dramatic," I sighed, crossing my arms over my chest since I was getting cold, too. "It's only been recently that I started to trust him enough to consider taking this step."

"He's been dating as much as you have," my bestie pointed out.

"He has, but like me, it's been half-hearted." Her brow went up in the air, and I held up my hand. "I believe him. What he said in so many words reflected my experiences with dating. He could never find someone who was just the right match. Everyone was always just a hair off-center."

She motioned at the door of the cooler. "Because the one who was the right match was standing right there the whole time!"

"You are quite excitable this morning," I said on a yawn. "How much coffee have you had."

"It has nothing to do with coffee and everything to do with the fact that I got eight hours of sleep because I wasn't boinking the baker!"

"Boinking the baker. I like that. I bet a chick could write a whole romance novel based on that title alone."

Amber lowered her brow at me and growled. "You're deflecting."

I held up my hands in defense. "I will not argue that I was boinking the baker, and all I'm going to say is, that boy knows how to knead."

Her eyes widened, and then laughter tumbled out until she had to sit down on the floor and lean against the door. "I can't tell you how thrilled I am right now. I knew something was up because I've rarely ever seen you like this."

"Like what?" I asked curiously.

"Happy. Really, truly, you can't bring me down, happy. I've seen it once before, and that was eight years ago when we opened the doors of The Fluffy Cupcake. I haven't seen it since. I'm so relieved to know he's going to take care of you now."

I took a step forward and knelt in front of her, sticking my finger in her chest. "I don't need anyone to take care of me, most especially a man!"

"Whoa, simmer down, Petunia," she whispered, using her childhood nickname for me. It's funny what happens when you pick someone else's petunias. You get a nickname for life. "I just meant sexually and maybe, eventually, your heart." Amber stood and hugged me tightly. "Brady told me he was worried he'd screwed it all up when he kissed you in the cooler."

"We talked about it, and he apologized. He promised it wouldn't happen again and that us sleeping together upstairs wouldn't change anything when we are downstairs."

She tucked my hair back behind my ears and straightened my apron. "Do you believe him?"

"Time will tell, but for the most part, I do. He's never been about his ego, and I don't see that changing now. He has had multiple opportunities to have issues being managed by two women, and he never has."

"No, he hasn't. I don't think he's wired that way. He's easy to work with because he's a team player. He isn't afraid to take criticism and work harder the next time to prove himself. Guys like him are hard to come by, as you know."

I nodded and took a deep breath, reminding myself that sleeping with Brady was completely different than being in a relationship with him. "I do know, and that probably helped me see that Brady's a different kind of man. He embraces what other men find off-putting—from my hips to my ass to the fact that I own a bakery. None of that fazes him."

Amber snorted and rolled her eyes to her hairline. "Not true. The hips and ass, those faze him. He hasn't taken his eyes off them all morning."

"That might be due to the promise I made him of a repeat performance tonight," I said on a wink as I pushed past her and threw the door open.

Brady stood by the door with his arms crossed. "I was worried. Your cupcakes almost burned."

"I knew you'd look out for my cupcakes," I said, hip-checking him on my way by to the oven. "But also," I tapped the timer clipped to the pocket of my coat.

He grinned and kept his arms crossed over his chest as I started pulling cupcakes out of the oven. "What are you doing?" I finally asked without making eye contact.

"Trying to remind myself this is my place of employment, and ravishing you here would be a bad idea."

"A terrible one," Amber said, coming out of the cooler with more cupcakes. "At least if I'm in the room."

All three of us laughed, but it was when Amber left that he stepped up to me and closed the oven door after the last pan was pulled. "She knows?"

"She refused to open the door until I told her," I admitted, my breath heavy with him so close to me. All I could think about was the way he felt warm against my thighs last night. "She could tell something had changed. It wasn't like I could lie to her when you keep staring at my ass like it's better than sliced bread."

Cupcake

"Well, it is," he said without pause. "Way better."

"Hey, baker man?"

"Yes, cupcake?"

I pointed at the oven. "While you've been busy ogling my ass, your buns are burning."

He jumped into action, pulling the buns out at the last second before they would be considered overdone, but not before he patted my ass.

I chuckled all the way back to the bench with my cupcakes in hand. "Maybe you're the one who needs a timer."

Fifteen

What the hell was going on? I set the piping bag down when I heard raised voices from the front of the bakery. It sounded like Amber could use some help with some unruly customers.

"I want the black forest cupcakes. If you don't give them to me, I'll report you to the Better Business Bureau!"

"That's not how the Better Business Bureau works," Amber said dryly. "Regardless, those cupcakes are for a special order, which is why they're neatly packaged and awaiting pick up."

"First come, first serve," the woman demanded.

I rolled my eyes. Why does Darla always have to show up and ruin a perfectly good day?

"Is there a problem here, ladies?" I asked, stepping behind the counter to stand next to Amber. We decided when the store first opened that we'd always show a united front with customers—giving them the idea that our alliance was to anything other than the business wasn't going to happen. Especially when that customer was Darla McFinkle.

"Yes, little Miss Fluffy Cupcake!" Darla exclaimed, tossing up her hands. Geez, this woman and her dramatics. How did she manage to get through life when she was always this worked up about things? "I want to purchase some black forest cupcakes and your business partner," which she said with a mouthful of acid, "won't let me!"

"Well, of course not. Those cupcakes are for a special order. They should be picking them up at any moment." I dramatically checked the clock, mostly to hide the smirk on my face.

"Too bad. I'm here, and I want cupcakes. They should have to wait for you to make more."

"Are you kidding me with this?" Amber asked, leaning forward on the counter with her palms. "The order was made three days ago and paid for already. Therefore, those cupcakes are already the property of the customer."

"Possession is nine-tenths of the law," Darla snarled.

This woman drove me crazy. She didn't want the damn cupcakes. She wanted to start a fight, draw attention to herself, and make us look bad.

"You're absolutely right, Darla," I said, nodding with her. I could see in her sarcastic smirk that she thought she'd won. "Since I'm in possession of those cupcakes, I get to make the decisions. They will go to the person who ordered and paid for them. Can I interest you in one of our Chocolate Heath cupcakes?"

"What I want is a black forest cupcake! Since your establishment is unable to provide for the customer what they want, I won't be frequenting it any longer." She spun in a huff on her heel toward the door.

The snort escaped before I could stop it. "Well, that's tragic. I'm sure I'll go home and cry about that for at least zero minutes. I might even crack open that bottle of champagne I've been saving for a special occasion."

"I'll join you," Amber said dryly.

Darla paused in her forward motion and spun back slowly, her jaw clenched and her hands fisted at her side. "You'll pay for that comment, fatso!" she exclaimed, lunging over the counter at me.

Before I could react, she had my hair in her hands and was yanking me over the counter by it. Spittle flew from her mouth like a rabid dog as she grappled with getting me over the counter, but Amber grabbed hold of my waist and screamed for help.

"Let her go before you hurt her!" she yelled, her voice frantic and worried.

"What is going on in here?" a voice asked. "Darla, let go of her right now!" Brady boomed from behind me while my scalp screamed for release.

Darla stopped pulling but didn't let go. "Back away, baker boy. This is between fatso and me. We don't need your help to solve this."

Brady walked into my line of sight and around the counter but didn't touch Darla. "I don't know what your problem is, but if you don't let go of Haylee this instant, you're going to have an even bigger problem on your hands."

Instead of releasing me, she pulled harder, forcing me to slide my stomach up onto the counter to stop her from ripping out my hair. I grasped her wrists, not wanting to fight back but afraid she was going to rip my hair out if I didn't do something.

"This ends now," another voice said from the doorway. "Release Chef Davis and put your hands behind your back," Officer Jack Stevens said, his gun belt clanking as he approached the still rabid woman. "If you don't release her now, I will arrest you for assault."

Darla's hands went slack, allowing me to stand upright again. I rubbed at my scalp, fighting back the tears in my eyes while I glared at the woman in front of me. Brady darted behind the counter and put his arm around my waist, checking my head for any damage.

"I don't think she hurt anything, but you can't let her get away with this," he whispered in my ear.

Darla was arguing with Officer Stevens when I tuned back into the space around me. "You can't arrest me! I didn't do anything," she whined, faking tears. "I wasn't going to hurt her."

"You could have fooled me," Brady said, his arm still around my waist.

"What? Are you two a thing now?" she asked, her eyes rolling. "What a shame. A guy like you with a woman like her. You could do so much better."

"I think it's time to take a trip down to the station," Officer Stevens said before I could leap over the counter and grab *her* this time. "Haylee, do you want to press charges?"

I shook my head slightly. "No. Just get her out of here. She's banned from The Fluffy Cupcake for good now. If she walks through that door again, I will call you, and I will press charges."

Darla started huffing and sputtering until she noticed the look on our faces. "Fine. You know what? Who cares? I don't need your stinking cupcakes! I can make my own!"

"You do that, Darla. Have a nice day. Thank you, Officer Stevens," I said cordially, biting my lip to keep from laughing at the dramatic woman.

"You better watch your back, fatso. If you think I don't have ways of making sure your business goes down in flames, you're wrong!"

"Whoa," Officer Stevens said, his hands reaching for his cuffs. "With that, we are taking a trip to the station." He slapped the cuffs on her wrists while she twisted and turned frantically. "I knew you were dumb, but threatening someone's place of business with arson in front of a peace officer is idiotic."

"I didn't! I didn't mean it like that!" Darla yelled on the way to the squad car.

All three of us stood frozen in place, staring at the door while Officer Stevens forced Darla into his squad car and drove away.

"Did that just happen?" Amber asked, the words filled with perplexed curiosity.

"It most certainly did," Brady said, turning me into him and hugging me fiercely. "I almost had a heart attack when I walked in here and saw you in a headlock. Do you need a doctor?" he asked, kissing the top of my head.

I shuddered in his arms but shook my head. "No, I'm fine."

"I can't believe that woman!" Amber sputtered, her senses returning. "What is wrong with her?"

"She's losing it," Brady said through clenched teeth. "Do you think they'll disqualify her for the cupcake bake-off now?"

I snorted and picked my hat up off the floor where it had fallen when she attacked me. "Not unless they charge her with something, which they won't. They know she will find a lawyer to get her off, and all it will do is make her even more insufferable."

"Let her show up and bake," Amber said, her eyes rolling. "She can't beat the dream team."

"Now we're the dream team?" I asked, joking with Brady.

"You're the girl of my dreams, how about that?" he asked with a teasing lilt to his voice.

"Oh sure, the fatso is your dream come true. Darla's right, you know, you could do so much better."

"You're both wrong, which we will discuss later, in private," he said, his lips in a thin line.

"I'm in Brady's camp, if that matters," Amber piped up. "No one is better than my bestie. I hope that's enough of a hint to him not to mess with you. He messes with you, and he messes with me."

Brady put his hands up by his chest. "I can read between the lines. Speaking of the cupcake bake-off," he said, to change the subject. "It's in less than a week. We need to do a few more run-throughs to make sure we're a well-oiled machine."

Amber shooed us to the back with her hands. "Why don't you two make another test batch while I clean up and wait for Mrs. Mack to pick up the coveted cupcakes?"

"Make a test batch so that you can eat them?" I asked teasingly.

"I'll be real with you. Yes. Also, add more marshmallow fluff this time to the frosting. Did you try adding it to the cake itself? I think that would be divine."

"What is this? The Great British Bake Off?" I asked, grabbing a clean apron from the hook on the wall.

"Don't knock it until you try it," she said, spun on her heel and disappeared back into the bakery to do her work.

"She might be onto something," Brady whispered, walking up to me and pulling me into him. "But I don't want to make cupcakes. I want to go upstairs with you and help you relax. Is your head okay?" He rubbed the sides of my head with his thumbs and then kissed my lips gently, grimacing when he remembered his promise not to kiss me in the bakery again. "I know I said I would stay hands off at work, but I was scared to death when I came around the corner and saw you in that bitch's grasp."

I chuckled and clasped his wrists with my hands. "It's okay. I won't tell the bakery police if you don't. As for my head, it's fine. I'm ticked off and shaking inside, but I'm not hurt physically. As much as I want to relax, I won't be able to. Let's whip up a batch of Berry Sinful, and maybe after I take my frustrations out on the cupcake batter, I'll feel better about the day."

He leaned down and kissed my nose. "I'm your guy then. Let's perfect this recipe so we can show Darla just what The Fluffy Cupcake is made of."

"Considering that's what she calls me," I said, leaving the sentence open.

"The bakery, not its baker," he clarified, his brow down to his nose. "I'm rather fond of the baker and happen to know there is nothing fluffy about her. She's all woman and all mine."

He went off to gather ingredients for the cake while I braced my palms on the bench and sucked in a few deep breaths. Darla had always been the bane of my existence, but if she ever threatened me or this business again, I would make sure she paid for it in ways she couldn't even fathom.

Sixteen

The woman lying next to me was warm, soft, and sleepy. I should probably leave her alone to sleep for a few more hours, but my appetite for her hadn't been sated yet. She was fire, sass, beautiful, vulnerable, and wicked good at making me come way before I wanted the romp to be over. The most wonderful and the most disturbing part was that she didn't even realize it. She doesn't believe she's the best thing since sliced bread, so I plan to show her over and over until she does. No matter what I have to do, this woman will know her worth is the same as Amber's, Darla's, and every other woman on the street, but she will understand that to me, she's worth more than all of them.

"Are you fondling my cupcake?" she asked in a sleepy voice.

"I wouldn't do that without your permission," I promised, taking a bite of the strawberry cupcake in my hand.

"I'm talking about the one in your hand, not the one between my legs," she said, laughter in her voice as she sat up.

"Then no, I'm not fondling the cupcake in my hand, but I was thinking about fondling the one between your legs."

"Again?" she asked with mock surprise.

I leaned over her, the cupcake still in my hand, and kissed her hard. My tongue darted in to taste her

126

sweetness that overpowered the cake. I moaned, and my dick hardened instantly at the thought of sinking deep inside her again.

"And again, and again and again," I promised when I lifted my head.

She grasped my wrist and brought the cupcake to her lips, stealing a bite of the sweet cake. "Mmm, berry sinful."

I leaned up against the headboard, naked as a jaybird with my dick at attention. "This part is brilliant." I pointed at the center filled with marshmallow fluff. "It reminds me of a Hostess cupcake when I was a kid. The cake and frosting were terrible, but you knew that creamy center was waiting for you." I stuck my tongue into the marshmallow and swirled it around, sucking and licking the cream from the center of the cupcake. "Mmm," I sighed with contentment. "I love sticking my tongue into the center of a cupcake."

Haylee's moan was low and almost a whine, but I heard it for what it was—desire. She squirmed next to me, her hand going down to rub her triangle as my tongue finished swiping out the center of the cupcake.

I grasped her hand and twined her fingers in mine. "Oh no, cupcake. Only one person gets to touch you there tonight. He's drooling at the thought of it, but first," I paused and held up a finger, grabbing another cupcake off the plate and holding it up.

"You're going to get sick if you eat more sugar," she moaned, squeezing my hand and then dropping it to try and get hers around my hardness.

"I'm not going to eat it," I said while I knelt next to her. My finger swiped through the frosting until it was full of it. "Well, I am going to eat it, but not the way you think. See, this icing is soft, fluffy, and sweet as can be." I ran my finger across both nipples until they were covered in icing. She shivered under me as it trailed to her navel. "Those three words sum up who you are, cupcake," I promised, grabbing more frosting to paint her beautiful naval and then lower until her entire mound was full of frosting.

"See, you do think I'm fluffy," she said, her brow drawn down to her nose. "I said you could do better, and you said I was wrong."

"You are wrong," I said, setting the cupcake down and holding my finger to her lips until she sucked my finger into her mouth and curled her tongue around it, sucking the frosting off. I moaned when the thought struck me how incredible it would feel if it was my dick instead.

I lowered my lips and did the same to her nipple until her hips were in the air, and she was begging me to take her. Before I switched to her other nipple, I grasped her chin with my fingers. "First of all, if what you are is fluffy, then I fucking love fluffy. I can't get enough of fluffy. My dick is hard and straining to be inside you again. If I thought I could do better, would I be this hard for you?" I asked, letting her squeeze me once before I pulled back and sucked her other nipple between my lips, licking and tugging until she was surely wetter than I'd ever made her. I trailed my tongue down and dipped it into her navel, swirling it around until she gasped and grabbed my hair with both hands.

"God, Brady," she sighed, her hips in the air until I grasped them and lowered them to the bed.

"I don't think soft is a problem, either. These hips and this ass are soft, and I love holding them while I pump into you." I licked my lips and eyed her core, still covered in frosting, and already plump from our earlier lovemaking. "I happen to love sweet things, and when you come all over my tongue, it's the sweetest thing I've ever tasted."

"Mmm, you're saying you don't think I'm a fatso, and you can't do better?"

I didn't answer her with words. I lowered my lips to her mound and systematically licked off every bit of frosting until I made my way to her slit. She was glistening with wetness, and while my tongue finished my snack, I slipped two fingers inside her and offered pressure where I knew she wouldn't be able to do anything but come the moment I touched my tongue to her.

"Brady," she cried, the spasm that hit her was almost instantaneous when I sucked her clit into my mouth. Her moans and mewls filled my head like an orchestra, and when she settled back into the bed, sated and happy, I rested my chin on her belly. "The sounds you make when you're coming are like listening to an orchestra play. Your moans fill my head and make me want to come without even touching myself. I don't want to fucking hear that we aren't perfect for each other ever again, do you understand me?" I asked, already rubbing her again until her gasp told me she was more than ready for me to enter her. "Do you understand me?" I asked again, poised with my tip at her opening.

"Yes," she cried, wrapping her legs behind me and pulling me forward until I slid inside her on a moan. "I understand you. Just fuck me, Brady."

I grasped her hips and moved inside her, carrying her up onto a fluffy cloud made of frosting, marshmallow, and the truth about who we are and what we can be together. My hips stroked hers until I couldn't hold back a second longer.

"Now," she called, her back arching off the bed and shoving her breasts into my face when I lowered myself over her to go even deeper. "Now, Brady!"

I grunted and came hard inside her, listening while she called my name over and over, her body shaking and spasming until she collapsed back to the bed in exhaustion.

I trailed my finger down her cheek and kissed her lips tenderly, mine sweet with frosting and her. "As it turns out, we are the dream team."

Her sleepy, sated smile told me she finally agreed.

Seventeen

The weather was beautiful and the day was bright and warm. I was ready to get my cupcake wars on, but first, we had to sit through a boring preliminary bake-off where the top three teams were chosen for the final round tomorrow.

"What do you think, can the dream team take them?" he asked with his lips near my ear.

I shivered where I stood by the mixer and tried not to melt into a puddle of sex on the floor. Brady had that effect on me every single time he got too close to me.

"I'm not even worried. Nice idea with the Hostess Cupcakes. Simple, nostalgic, and fun."

"True, but they wouldn't be from The Fluffy Cupcake if they didn't have a twist," he said, winking at me while he finished mixing the frosting.

I busied myself with preparing the finished cupcakes for filling and icing while keeping my eye on the other entrants. There were seven, some teams, some individuals, and all of them were scrambling to finish their cupcakes in the ten minutes we had left. Some had just taken them from the oven, which meant their frosting was going to be a drippy mess when presented to the judges. Since we weren't allowed to make the same recipe twice, we saved the Berry Sinful ones for tomorrow and used the classic chocolate cupcakes to secure our spot in the top three today. Blocking the other teams, especially Darla, who was working alone, from seeing what I was doing, I grabbed the pastry bag and piped in the filling. Brady then expertly iced the cupcake with the chocolate dip icing and piped on the white squiggle. We only needed three cupcakes, so when they were finished, I checked the clock. We had three minutes to spare. While everyone else was running around like desperate chickens avoiding the chopping block, I calmly set the three cupcakes in front of the judges, smiled, chuckled at a joke Mr. Samson told me, and then walked back to my station to help Brady clean up.

Daggers hit my back, and I turned to see Darla glaring at me like I was the devil incarnate. It had been a week since her tirade in my bakery, and she had been smart enough to stay away. I suspected if Darla didn't get into this bake-off, my peace would end here. She'd have nothing to lose then, at least in her mind. Except if Darla showed back up in my bakery, Brady would have her arrested. She didn't believe I'd do it, but I knew without a doubt that he would.

We loaded the dirty dishes and bowls into a bin and set it on the cart. Brady pushed it over to the area marked for storage while we waited for everyone else to finish. We'd load it in the van later and take all the dishes back to the bakery to wash. The way Darla was eyeing Brady on his way back to our table told me she was plotting how to steal him away from me. The last few weeks ran through my mind and brought a smile to my face. He was way too addicted to my cupcake for that to work, but she was delusional enough to believe she could. When it came to what Darla thought about herself, she was every man's dream.

"Stop obsessing about McFinkle," Brady said out the corner of his lip while we waited for the judges' verdict. "She's not even worth the thought you've given her in the last three minutes."

"I'm just worried she'll do something stupid, and you'll have to kick her ass."

He snorted with laughter, his eyes twinkling with amusement. "I don't hit women, but I'm not afraid to throw her out of the bakery by her ear. Your ass, on the other hand, I'd happily grasp, if we weren't in public."

"My ass and I thank you," I said, laughing, which only seemed to make Darla angrier. "She really can't stand to see other people happy, can she?" I asked, a fake smile on my face.

"People like that usually can't because they aren't happy. She doesn't want anyone else to be either."

"Bakers, we have reached a decision," Mr. Samson said from the judges' table. "While all the entries were fantastic, the rules say we have to trim the teams down to three. With a delightfully light sponge cupcake, Darla McFinkle will move on to the final round."

Clapping ensued, and Darla preened like a beauty queen accepting her crown. It took everything I had to keep from rolling my eyes, but the judges were watching.

"After submitting a wonderful strawberry creamsicle cupcake, Team Barton will be on to the final round."

More clapping and I swallowed around the lump in my throat. There was no way the owner of the cupcake business wasn't going to make it to the final round, was there?

"The final entrant, offering a beautiful throwback to our childhood with their strawberry filled Hostess cupcake, is Team Fluffy Cupcake!"

The rest of the teams clapped wildly, and I figured the other teams were probably glad someone was going to give Darla a run for her money if it couldn't be them. I let the breath out I'd been holding and smiled a real smile—the first one all day.

"Thank you for judging the competition today. I'm glad you enjoyed the cupcake. It just might make it into the bakery case soon," I said when I shook hands with the judges as they came around to the tables. Once they'd congratulated everyone, Mr. Samson grabbed the microphone.

"Remember, the bake-off starts tomorrow at one o'clock sharp. You'll have thirty minutes to prep your ingredients beforehand, but you cannot mix anything until the clock starts. Once it's running, you'll have ninety minutes to complete the cupcake, exactly as entered on your form, other than your secret ingredient, and present them to the judges. The judges then have one hour to make their final decision and crown the cupcake winner. Any questions?"

We all shook our heads since we'd been through this every year for at least six. While the teams who made it to the final round every year changed, the rules never did, and I had them memorized long ago. Tomorrow morning I'd be putting all my ingredients in individual containers at the bakery. The judges checked everyone's supplies before the time started, so as long as I followed the no mixing rule, being prepared when I arrived wasn't against the rules. Once the clock started, all I had to do was begin the mixing. If I didn't have everything ready to grab and go when the timer started, the cupcakes wouldn't be cool enough to frost in our allotted time, as many of the teams learned today.

We had the process down to less than ninety minutes because Brady and I were a great team. That was something I would have known sooner if I'd let him break through my tough exterior years ago instead of holding everyone at bay to protect my heart. I will say, with much reluctance, that my heart was as smitten with Brady as my body was. I just wasn't entirely sure what to do about it. I didn't want to tell him that and ruin whatever we had going when he didn't feel the same. I could enjoy the fling for what it was, I suppose, but my birthday was crawling closer with every sunset and sunrise. So, while that red X was no longer visible on the calendar, I could still see it in my mind's eye.

"Congratulations, Team Fluffy Cupcake," Darla said when she passed our table on the way up the aisle. "I hope you bring your A-game tomorrow because I have the winning recipe this year. Don't count me out of this competition just yet."

"Wouldn't dream of it, Darla," Brady said while I ignored her completely. It was smarter to do that than say something that would only serve to get me into hot water with her, or worse yet, disqualified from the competition.

"The sass with that one is strong," Brady said as she strut away like the prima donna she is.

"I would like to forget she exists. At least until I have to see her again tomorrow."

Brady grinned and untied his apron from around his waist, his trim hips making my mouth water. Since it was July and nearly eighty degrees, we decided to wear shorts with our bakery coats. I wasn't in the mood to sweat to death, and to be honest, I loved nothing more than him in shorts. His were the color of sand and the texture of seersucker. I was a sucker for everything about him if I was honest with myself. I also had a thing for a nice pair of man calves. Does that make me weird? Probably. Moving on.

"I think we should have a little fun at the fair. What do you think? There won't be any time tomorrow, and there's a pronto pup out there with my name on it somewhere," he was saying when I tore my gaze from his legs.

I tossed my apron in our bin and snapped the lid on it, glad our work was done. "I'm game. Let's stash this in the van and head out. First, we better check on Amber."

He grabbed the cart and followed me out of the convention center and toward the van. We locked everything in the back before heading for the food tent, where Amber was stationed with a wide variety of bread, buns, and cupcakes from the bakery, including our strawberry cupcakes à la Hostess. Tomorrow, the crowd would get their first taste of Berry Sinful after the competition was over. Win or lose, I knew the cupcakes were going to be favorites with the community during the summer months.

When we arrived, the tent was less crowded than the one that held all the hot food, which was okay. It was hard to drool over loaves of bread and piles of cupcakes when you couldn't get near the booth to check out the selection. What I saw when I found our booth stopped me dead in my tracks. There were two loaves of bread and a tray of cupcakes left. Everything else was gone.

"Amber!" I exclaimed, jogging around the end of the table to hug her. "What the heck happened here?"

She was already laughing before she spoke. "I swear, Haylee, everyone wants a taste of your fluffy cupcakes!"

"Too bad," Brady growled under his breath, "She's all mine."

I snorted, and Amber rolled her eyes, the shine of us getting together having worn off the second week we spent *making googly eyes at each other*, as she put it. While she was kidding, we did try to keep our relationship, to whatever extent that was, to a minimum at the bakery, just like we'd promised each other. It was easy right now. We were too busy to worry about anything other than getting our orders done. It would get harder if this lasted into winter when the tourists left, and we didn't have as much to do every day.

"Someone tried the new chocolate cupcake, started telling everyone about it, and they were like a pack of rabid wolves in here. It was something else. I was afraid I was going to lose a finger."

"But the question is, did people actually like them once they got one in their paw?" I asked, leaning my hip on the table.

"I'm telling you—it was like nirvana around here the way people's eyes were rolling around in their heads when they took a bite. If we could package that feeling and sell it, we'd be rich."

"Well, we can," Brady said from the other side of the table. "It's called cupcakes in a box. Voila."

Amber and I both chuckled. He was right. I was thrilled to hear that they had gone over so well. "I'm honestly surprised. Usually, you have the people who love Hostess cupcakes and the people who can't stand them. There's very few who sit on the fence about them."

Amber pointed at me. "I had many who bought them so they could complain about how fake they tasted blah, blah," she said, waving her hand. "One bite, and they were moaning along with everyone else. The Able Baker Brady cakes gave people that feeling of being a kid again, but also they pleased their more grownup palate."

"The Able Baker Brady cakes?" Brady asked with skepticism, and she nodded. "That's what I started calling them. They were your idea, after all."

I nodded and winked at him. "They were your idea and a damn good one. We need to make another batch to sell tomorrow then," I said right away. "People can fill up on those until we break out the Berry Sinful samples."

"We can whip them up fast in the morning," Brady agreed. "We don't have to be here until one, and we don't have any special orders for the morning, which we did on purpose. The lack of bread here is a problem we have to address, though."

Amber spun to face him. "They heard that Able Baker Brady's bread was on display, and they all wanted to poke a loaf or two." Brady and I burst out laughing at the same time, our shoulders shaking until Amber couldn't hold it in either. "You two are sickos!"

Brady glanced at the two loaves left on the table. "It looks like all the kitschy flavors are gone."

"Kitschy," Amber said, laughing, "exactly what everyone was calling them, too."

"You know what I mean," he said with laughter filling his voice. "I'll make more of those tonight and worry less about the others. There will only be so much time, even if I go in a few hours early."

"You know what they say," Amber said on a wink. "Better to leave them wanting more and knowing where to get it than wear them all out in a weekend."

I hugged her one last time and walked back around the table where Brady put his arm around me. "I didn't know anyone said that. As for me, I'm all about being worn out all weekend."

We walked out of the tent with grins on our faces and her laughter filling our ears.

Eighteen

The fair was bustling. There were families with young kids and the elderly wandering down the paths to check out the displays. Later tonight, when the midway opened, the teens and young people would flood the place. I was glad I would be at home sleeping. Haylee took a bite of her pronto pup and moaned softly, garnering a look from me as we walked toward a bench under a tree.

"This reminds me of my teenage years," she said, licking mustard off her lip. It was my turn to release a soft moan because I wanted to do the licking.

"You came to the fair a lot as a kid?" I asked, licking my lips of the ketchup I'd put on my dog.

"I worked here as a teenager. All the fair food you could eat and six bucks an hour cash. It was every kid's dream. My hips and ass are proof."

My eyes drifted to her lower half. "Remind me to thank the fair before we leave."

She snickered and lowered herself to the bench, our early morning catching up to her. We were used to working early and long hours, but working those hours and then baking all afternoon added to the fatigue we were already fighting. Of course, if we stopped making love all night and got some sleep, that might help. That wasn't nearly as much fun, though. As much as I hated the idea, we'd have to leave soon and head back for a nap before we had to bake again tonight.

"We should head home," Haylee said, finishing her food. "We need to be baking again in," she checked her watch, "eight hours."

"Can we spend those next eight hours in your bed?" I asked, tossing our garbage in a can and sitting next to her to people watch.

"Only if our eyes are closed, and we're not wrapped around each other."

"Zero out of ten, do not recommend."

She laughed, her head tossed back as it shook back and forth with her beautiful brown hair gleaming in the sunshine. "You are too much, Able Baker Brady."

"Where did this Able Baker Brady thing come from?" I asked, perplexed.

When she turned to me, her face was filled with shock. "You know, Able Baker Charlie from the Richard Scarry books?"

My head tipped to the side. "Uh, no, but I didn't have your typical childhood."

She nodded, her eyes clouding over for a moment. "I didn't either, but when I moved in with Amber, she made sure I had all those experiences I missed out on as a kid. We watched the cartoon shows that I wasn't exposed to before, and read books that were silly when you were fifteen, but helped me understand why people held them in their hearts so dearly. We watched old movies like E.T. and Back to the Future, and listened to music from the eighties. She even made me work with her at the fair, so I could experience what other kids took for granted. I wasn't a fan of the midway, it did nothing for my stomach, but the food?" She rubbed her belly and grinned. "I appreciated the hell out of that experience. The fair is the reason I became a chef."

"Seriously?" I asked in shock. "I guess you've never said what brought you to that decision."

She motioned out across the open field they used for showing animals and at the barn beyond. "Every year, the kids who were in 4-H, and women in home economic groups, submitted items to the fair to be judged, right?" she asked, and I nodded. "I loved going to the barn at the end of every shift to see what had been added. Some of the meringue pies were fabulous, Brady. Seriously, it took me years to learn how to make a meringue stand up like that. I was fascinated by it and started experimenting at home. Trust me, Amber's family never argued about tasting my experiments. When I graduated from high school, the idea of becoming a chef never crossed my mind. I just wanted a stable career, so I never had to worry about where my next meal was coming from again."

"Which you wouldn't have had to if you'd become a chef," I said on a chuckle.

"I was eighteen, out on my own for the first time and scared. That never filtered into my brain, Brady."

"Understandable. Let me guess. You chose business."

She pointed at me with a grin. "I did. I went to St. Paul College for business and needed to find a job quickly that would work around my school schedule. I got hired on at a little bakery called A Pinch and A Dash. I worked with the owner, Mr. Hennington, who was just the sweetest guy I'd ever met. He was about seventy when he took me under his wing and didn't just ask me to do the work. He taught me to do the work. He taught me to love it and respect the process. I think I was in school about a month when I was sitting in Business Principles 101, and it hit me. I wanted to be a baker. I changed my major to culinary arts to learn the basics while still working with Mr. Hennington. I took a few business classes at night, so I could successfully run a bakery and get my master baker certificate. The rest is history."

I put my arm around her and kissed her temple, the emotions welling inside me for the woman I was head over heels for, I had come to realize. "Your history is pretty damn successful, too. What you've done to build the business to where it is today is almost unheard of by someone your age."

She leaned into me and rested her head on my shoulder. "Thank you, but I had help. Amber is in charge of the marketing, and you know she's a genius at it. My success at The Fluffy Cupcake hasn't come without expense to my personal life. I haven't had one to any extent, and I'm almost thirty. I guess that's why I made that stupid red X on my calendar this year. I wanted to hold myself accountable to start etching out time for more than work."

"When we're together, does it feel like you have to etch out time? It sure doesn't feel that way to me."

"That's the weirdest part," she whispered. "When we're together, it's natural. Like—"

"It's meant to be," I finished, kissing her then to keep her from saying anything more. I kept the kiss light and close-lipped, considering we were in the middle of the county fair, but I wanted her to remember how natural it felt to be with me. I ended the kiss and gazed into her eyes, all her hopes and dreams laid out in them for me to see. "We should probably head back and get some rest. Your eyes tell me you're tired."

"How do my eyes tell you I'm tired?" she asked, standing when I gave her my hand and helped her up.

"When you're tired, all the walls you keep up around yourself drop and your eyes turn the color of weak coffee. I can see right through them to everything you want, but don't think you deserve. While I love seeing your hopes and dreams reflected at me, I also know those walls protect you from a lot of things in this world that you're not prepared to deal with just yet. I don't want one of those things to blindside you when you aren't prepared."

I kept my arm around her waist, and she rested her head on my shoulder while we walked up the midway toward the parking lot where we'd left the bakery van. Every few feet, we had to stop and talk to someone we knew or wave at someone working at one of the food booths. Lake Pendle was a small town, and when it came to Strawberry Fest, everyone pitched in.

Cupcake

"You're quiet," I said as we approached the 4-H building.

"You blindsided me with the statement about the walls, and eyes, and being blindsided."

"I'm sorry?" I asked, stopping and leaning her up against the wall of the building. "That wasn't what I was trying to do."

She waved her hand in the air. "I know, and I'm not upset. You don't have to apologize. It's weird hearing it from someone else in that way, I guess. I always thought I did a good job of hiding my demons."

"You do when you're rested, but not when you're tired. I just want you to know you don't have to hide your demons with me. If you get upset and scared, you can yell at me, call me names, tell me to leave you alone, or whatever you need to do, and I will understand why. I will let you do those things because sometimes we all need someone to carry our burdens for a little while."

"Will you leave me alone?" she asked, staring at the ground instead of my eyes.

I tipped her chin up with my finger until our gazes met again. "Never. I don't care how much you yell and scream, stomp your foot, or point at the door. I will give you space, but I won't leave you alone. I'll run you a bath and fill it with a lavender bubble bath and help you in. I'll hand you a glass of wine, and while you soak, I'll make you the most epic French toast you've ever had. After you eat, I'll massage your neck and back while you watch your favorite chick flick or talk about whatever is bothering you. Either way, you'll know I'm there beside you, silently supporting you through whatever it is that's causing you turmoil."

"That's awfully sweet of you, Brady," she said, letting her finger trail down my cheek. "I'd do the same for you. Minus the lavender bubble bath, of course."

I smiled and tossed her a wink before my lips claimed hers again for a hot second. "The only thing I need when I'm full of turmoil is you, a cupcake, and your bed. I'm a simple man that way."

Her laughter floated on the air as we started walking again toward the car. "Hey, do you want to dart in and look at the 4-H entries before we go home, or are you too tired?"

I motioned at the door of the barn. "Lead on, pretty lady. I love this part of the fair as much as you do. I did 4-H as a kid, once I moved in with my foster parents, and won the bread division every year. My ribbons are still a source of pride for me to this day."

She bumped me in the shoulder and grinned up at me. "I bet you knocked their socks off with your basil and dill pickle bread."

I laughed with her as we walked around the edges of the barn where the tables sat filled to the brim with pies, cakes, cookies, tarts, and bread. To say I was impressed was an understatement.

I pointed at one of the tables that held decorated theme cakes for birthdays. "I think we might be missing out on a source of labor in the community."

She was inspecting a Harry Potter cake when she glanced up at me. "What do you mean?"

"Think about it. These kids are already extremely talented. We could be bringing one or two into the bakery a few times a week for extra help and to teach them more about the process of baking in a large business like The Fluffy Cupcake."

"You mean as apprentices?"

"Sure, or as part-time help if they want the work. Either way, if they're in the bakery, they're learning life skills before they go off to college."

"Or they stay and work their way up to master baker," she said, gazing at the cakes spread out before us. "I like the way you think, Brady. I think we should come back tomorrow after the judging is done and write down the names of the winners. We ask one pastry baker and one bread baker if they'd be interested. If they say no, we move to the second-place winner. What do you think?"

My grin must have covered my entire face when I answered her. "I'm all in! I would love to pass on some of the knowledge I learned over the years as a way to repay the bakers who taught me about the craft. That includes you," I promised, kissing her nose. "But for now, we better get home, or Amber will have our heads when we don't get all the cupcakes baked for the morning."

She nodded once. "And you don't mess with Amber when it comes to cupcake selling."

We strode toward the door of the barn but stopped short near a room full of people. There was a woman on the stage, and she was giving an oratory about fashion.

"What is going on?" I asked, searching for a sign to indicate why Darla was up there talking about mini-skirts and leather jackets. I spotted the sign at the same time Haylee gave a derisive snort next to me. "Strawberry Fest Princess," I read aloud. "Are you kidding me? She's running for Strawberry Fest Princess after what happened in the bakery the other day?" My voice was a little loud, and a few of the people in the back of the room turned to glare at us.

We shrunk back and headed for the door again, with Haylee's arm slung through mine and laughter on her lips. "Darla will run for anything if it means the spotlight is on her."

"How does someone her age run for Strawberry Fest Princess?" I asked, confused.

"As long as you're single, you can enter the competition. Is it meant for the young girls of Lake Pendle? Sure, but until they change the rules, you can be ninety-five and enter as long as you've never been married."

"God knows she will still be running at ninety-five then," I muttered.

Haylee grinned and leaned her head on my shoulder. "Today is the interview and oratory portion and tomorrow night they hold the pageant. We can go watch if you want to."

"I would rather clean out the grease trap at the bakery on a Friday night than watch that witch prance around on a stage. Besides, how is she going to do that when she has to bake cupcakes in the afternoon? She'll barely have time to put on her ballgown and get on stage."

"Don't you know?" my cupcake asked with laughter in her voice. "Witches wear the same gown to everything."

Just when I thought I couldn't love her more, she reminded me that I could. The fact that I'd finally come to terms with the idea that I loved her wasn't as startling as I expected it to be. Gazing down at her beautiful face turned pink by the sunshine told me it was time to admit that truth to her, too. I had to take the next step. I just hoped she was ready to walk beside me.

Nineteen

Night had fallen, and the stars were out when we left my apartment to start baking. It was relatively early at one a.m., but with the bake-off later today, we had a lot of ground to cover. We wouldn't be open since the bakery had a booth at the fair, but we still needed goodies to sell at the booth. Able Baker Brady refused to make any of his artisan bread a day ahead, which meant we had to do it tonight. I couldn't blame him. No one would be happy with day-old bread when they were expecting fresh from the oven.

"Come here," he said, grabbing my hand and dragging me away from the doorway of the bakery and across the street.

"Brady, we need to get to work," I said, looking behind me as he dragged me up the street.

"We will, but we have plenty of time. I want to show you something," he said, his hand warm and tight in mine.

The lake came into view, and I shook my head in exasperation. "I've seen the lake before, Brady."

"I know you have, but have you seen it at one a.m. when the stars look like they're touching the water and the moon has rested its beam across the glassy surface."

"Well, when you put it like that," I said on a sigh as he pulled me under a giant oak tree with an overhang nearly to the ground. "It is pretty amazing," I said, gazing out at it

145

as he held me from behind, his back against the tree and me tight to his chest. "You can almost count the stars."

His hand shot out at a light that was streaking through the sky. I followed his finger as he moved it toward the water. "Make a wish on the shooting star."

I leaned my head back against his shoulder and sighed. "I think my wish came true already. I was just too stupid to realize it sooner."

"What was your wish?" he asked, nuzzling my neck.

"To find someone to seriously date by the time I was thirty."

"Seriously date?" he asked in confusion. "Versus?"

"Casually date or whatever," I said, suddenly unsure of myself.

"Are we seriously dating, cupcake?"

I turned and slapped my hand against his chest. "Why do you keep calling me cupcake when I tell you all the time to stop? It's very disrespectful," I said, changing the subject, incredibly self-aware that I'd put my foot in my mouth again.

"I'm not being disrespectful when I call you cupcake. I'm doing what I said I'd do from the beginning."

"Piss me off?" I asked, confused.

He smiled and kissed the tip of my nose. "No, show you your worth."

"And calling me cupcake, when it's a derogatory name I don't like, accomplishes that?"

"Let me ask you this. How do you feel when Darla calls you a fluffy cupcake?"

"Angry, sad, disrespected, and undeserving of my success."

He grasped my hand and held it to his chest. "All valid feelings, I agree. How do you feel when I say, *fuck me harder, cupcake* in your ear every night?"

I squirmed, but he wouldn't let go of my hand or let me turn away. "I guess I feel the opposite. Happy, respected, and deserving of your time and attention."

"How do you feel when I teasingly say, pass me the flour, cupcake?"

"The same?" I asked, and he grasped my chin, planting a light kiss on my lips.

"Question or statement?"

"Statement," I said. "I know that's how I feel, but I don't know where this is going."

"It's going exactly where I wanted it to go. I call you cupcake to show you that depending on who says it, and in what way, you can have different emotions about it. If you let Darla's connotation of the name be the only emotions you feel, then she wins. If you let my connotation of the name be the only emotions you feel, then you win. I call you cupcake because I respect the hell out of you, Haylee Davis. To me, when I call you that, it's a name filled with the utmost love and respect. That said, if you still don't like it, I'll stop."

I swung my head back and forth a few times, trying to blink back the tears in my eyes from his sweet admission. "Now that you've explained it, I see very plainly what you were doing. I just didn't realize how much it would matter to me to hear your explanation." I leaned my head against his shoulder, and he hugged me, his lips finding my ear to kiss before his teeth tugged on the lobe. "Wait. Love and respect?" I asked, lifting my head to stare into his eyes. "You meant that in a friend kind of way, right?"

He shook his head, barely enough for me to notice. "No, I meant in the I love you, kind of way, Haylee. It took me about one second after I kissed you to know that the crush I'd had on you all these years wasn't about sex. I know you felt it, too. It was fire." I nodded, swallowing hard when he balanced his forehead against mine. "When I realized that kissing you in the bakery made you nervous, I just wanted to make it right. I wanted you to know that I respected you and your business. When I sank into you the first time that night, God," he whispered, his eyes gazing at my lips. "I was just a goner, cupcake. Still am. Always will be for you."

Rather than let me speak, his lips captured mine in what I expected to be a hard kiss of desire and passion. Instead, it was gentle, flowing, and rippling like the lake behind us while he showed me with his body that his words were true.

He loved me.

His thumbs stroked my temple when he pulled back to gaze into my eyes. His blue ones were wide open and searching. "I know you don't feel the same way, but I'm hoping that given enough time, you will fall in love with me the way I have with you."

My head tipped to the sky that peeked at me from between the leaves of the tree. I laughed happily, which he wasn't expecting. His fingers tightened against my hips, whether to hold me there or to make sure I didn't fall, I wasn't sure.

"Brady, I do love you. I'm just terrible at showing it. I always have been. You have to understand that I don't know ho—"

His lips silenced mine, and he flipped me around, pinning me up against the tree and shoving his tongue inside my mouth. His passion ignited, I was going to have to ride his wave until it ebbed back out into the middle of the lake. There was no talking to him when his dick was a hard rod against my belly, and his tongue was most of the way down my throat.

He ripped his lips from mine and buried his face in my neck, a moan low on his lips. His hips thrust against my belly to relieve his pain while he suckled my neck for a breath. "You're so fucking incredible," he whispered, inhaling deeply. "Beautiful, talented, and you do things to me no one ever has before." He sucked gently at my collarbone for a moment while a shudder traveled through him. He would leave a mark, but my chef's coat would cover it, so I didn't stop him. Instead, I buried my hands in his hair and brought his lips back to mine.

"I love you, Brady," I whispered again. "Why did we wait so long to admit it?"

He cupped my cheek and smiled, his forehead coming down to rest against mine. "You were scared, and I understood that. I'm done waiting, though, do you understand?" I heard his zipper chatter as it went down, and then his dick was hard and bobbing against the front of my pants.

"Brady, put that away! We're in public."

His laugh was naughty, steamy, and sexy in a way I'd never heard before. "Stick with me, kid. You'll have lots of new experiences. The first is making love by the lake up against a tree. We're the only ones here besides the geese and the fish."

He kissed me, his lips anxious, and his hands busy. He pried my lips open again with his tongue and worked my pants down with his hands. What the hell were we doing? We were going to get caught, and I'd be the one with my pants around my ankles. Then again, he'd be the one with his dick hanging out. Someone would have to be walking right in front of the tree to see us, but it still felt carnal.

His hand traveled to my core, where I was already dripping wet for him. He rubbed to the rhythm of his tongue in my mouth, and when I was nearly coming in his arms, he pushed me up against the tree and entered me, our heights, and hearts, perfectly aligned.

I grasped his shoulders while he held my hips and drove himself into me. "I'm not going to last long," I hissed, the sensations different than any I'd ever felt before. This was more primal, and when he thrust forward, he sent zaps of electricity through me, dragging a moan from my lips each time. "I'm going to come, Brady," I cried, my body starting to shake from the pleasure building within my core.

He wrapped his arms around me and held me to him in a hug, so I pressed my face into his coat and came with his name on my lips, muffled but none less powerful.

"Haylee," he sighed, his chin over my shoulder as I shuddered in his arms. My muscles rippled over him in synchronized rhythm, and he rose up on the balls of his feet and thrust upward deeper, harder—burying himself over and over, dragging out my orgasm while his started to build. "Fuck, I can't stop," he moaned. Then he filled me with his love and tenderness until my orgasm pulled every last drop of him into me.

Brady fell back to his heels, and a sound ripped from his throat that could only be described as satisfied. "I'll never get enough of you, cupcake," he promised while he tucked himself back inside his pants and zipped them, then worked mine up and over my ass, after copping a feel. "How was your first quickie in the park?"

"Orgasmic," I said on a chuckle. I stroked his cheek with my thumb until he leaned back in for a kiss.

"For the record," he whispered, his forehead braced against my shoulder. "You're not terrible at showing your love. I felt all of it just now when you trusted me enough to let yourself go under a tree in a public park. That will always be enough for me. You will always be enough for me."

I nodded, a smile tipping my lips up. "I just want to be happy for the first time in my life. You make me happy. That tells me something in here," I said, tapping my chest.

"I hope it tells you that I'd do anything for you, be anything you need me to be, and protect you at all costs. Can I ask you something?" I nodded, a question in my eye. "Will you be my girlfriend? Like officially? Can I finally tell people that I'm dating the spectacular Haylee Davis?"

"I would love to be your girlfriend," I whispered, my heart melting with his question. "At least when we're upstairs or out here. In the bakery, I'm still your boss."

He laid a kiss on me then that had my lips stinging from the intensity and heat. "Downstairs, you're the boss of me. Upstairs, I'm the boss of you when we're in that bed. I can accept those terms," he hissed, his hands grasping my ass tightly.

"Hey, that's not what I said!" I exclaimed, pushing against his chest while he laughed.

"You're right, but that's what I heard. You and I both know that's the best of both worlds. You in my arms every night, and your sweet ass nestled against my belly as we sleep. If I have that, I'm happy forever."

I wrapped my arms around his neck and sighed. "Me, too. I love you," I said on a whisper as the breeze stole my words and carried them out across the water to be blessed by the moonbeam and the waves.

"Not as much as I love you," he promised. "But Amber won't love either of us if we don't get to work."

I straightened my clothes then followed him out from under the tree. "I know you're right, but I don't have to like it."

He slung his arm around me again as we made the trip back to the bakery quickly. "I'll do the bread while you do the cupcakes. We'll be done in no time, and we can catch a nap before the competition," he promised, a kiss to my temple while I unlocked the door of the bakery.

"Well, now you've jinxed us for sure," I teased, rubbing my ass against his groin on my way by him to the cooler to grab the first round of cupcakes.

The moan that tore from him filled me with unparalleled satisfaction.

Twenty

The bakery was quiet, which wasn't something I could say often. There was no hum of the mixer, ding of the bell over the door, or chatter by the counter. It was just me preparing the bins we'd need to take with us to the fairgrounds while Brady ran upstairs to shower.

Upstairs.

In my bathroom.

It felt strange but oddly perfect. Sure, Brady's apartment was across town, and it made more sense for him just to shower upstairs, but after our discussion last night, I wondered how long it would be before we took the next step in our relationship. How long do you wait to move in with each other? He's been at my apartment every night for the last couple of weeks, but that's just the newness of the relationship, right?

"Haylee, are you here?" Amber called as she walked into the bakery.

"How long are you supposed to date before you move in together?" I blurted out.

She paused in the doorway and looked left and then right. "Um, that depends?"

My shoulders slumped, and I shook my head. "Ignore me. I'm tired and have way too much on my mind."

"That much was clear," she said with a chuckle while she gave me one of her best friend hugs of encouragement. "Are you talking about you and Brady?"

"That obvious, eh?"

"Well, he does make googly eyes at you all day long, so pretty dang obvious, yeah."

"He told me he loved me last night and asked me to be his girlfriend," I whispered, looking around to make sure he hadn't come in the back door.

Amber grasped my shoulders and shook me. "What?" she exclaimed with so much excitement it didn't even sound like a question. "Seriously?" I nodded, my head on a string. "Oh, my heavenly cupcakes! What did you say?"

I laughed at her dramatics and gave her the palms out. "I told Brady that I'm bad at showing it, but I love him, too. I also agreed to be his girlfriend everywhere but here."

"Here, you're his boss," she said on a laugh. "I'm so frigging happy right now I can't even stand it."

"Wait," I said, sticking a pin in the conversation. "Why are you here?"

"I forgot the banner for the Berry Sinful cupcakes. I ran back to grab it before things get too busy over there. Taylor is handling the table until I get back."

"Why didn't you text me? I could have brought it with me."

"You could have, but it's slow over there right now, and I wanted to make sure you didn't need any help. Besides, Taylor is running the table so I can be fluid today. I need to help you and Brady with the bake-off and then run back here and grab all the Berry Sinful cupcakes you made for after the competition."

"They're finished if you want to take them now," I said, pointing at the cooler.

Her head swung side to side. "No way. I'm not risking Darla getting her hands on them and ruining our business. They'll stay locked up here until you're ready to reveal them."

"True, I hadn't thought of that. Darla would try it if she thought she could get away with it. Besides, it's going to be hot today, and the frosting won't hold up well if we don't keep them cold."

"She'd try anything to make herself look better since she knows you're going to win the competition again."

I shrugged and shifted uncomfortably. "Probably, and for that reason, I've decided this will be our last year in the bake-off."

"Um, what now?" she asked, checking my forehead for a fever.

I jokingly pushed her away and leaned on the bench. "I haven't said anything to Able Baker Brady yet, but I feel like it's time. It was Darla who mentioned it, sarcastically, of course, but it got me thinking."

"What did she mention?"

"She said it was getting a little tired that the professionals were always winning the bake-off. It was never meant to be a competition for professionals when it started, and when I first competed, I wasn't. To be honest, winning isn't even fun anymore."

Amber's eyes rolled in her head, and she scoffed. "Oh, heaven forbid you have that seal of approval in the window of your bakery every year. It's bad for business."

"The thing is, Amber, we don't need it anymore. We've been at this a few weeks shy of eight years, and we have more business than we can handle as it is. While bragging rights are fun, I want others to have a chance at them."

"Even if those others are Darla McFinkle?"

I brushed my hand at her in response. "Honestly, I doubt she will ever win, but if she does, more power to her. I think the only reason she competes is that she wants to beat me. Regardless, I have other plans. I need to talk to you about them, but after the fair is over when things aren't so hectic. That's another reason, actually. I want to enjoy the fair, and I can't do that with the bake-off and the business."

Her head tipped to the side. "What other plans?"

I sighed because I could see I wasn't getting away without some mention of them. "Brady and I were in the 4-H barn, and we were more than a little impressed with some of the entries. He suggested maybe we aren't utilizing talent in the community the way we could or should be. We're talking about using apprentices, one with each of us. There's a lot to explore there before we implement anything, but I like the idea. I think it's worth investigating."

She pointed at me with a nod. "I do, too. I was considering it for the front end with some of the Future Business Leaders of America kids. They work hard, and we could give them real-world experience to get them better prepared for college."

After a smile, I hugged her for a moment. "I love how we still think the same even after all these years. Once the fair is over, I'm going to make brownies, and we're all going to sit down together and hash these changes out. Our eighth year is going to be our best one yet!"

"I know that's because you're happy. Like really happy. All the time. That's due to the man upstairs, and I don't mean God. I mean Brady. As for the question you asked me when I walked in, I don't know the answer to that. I'm not even in a relationship."

"Which we have to fix," I pointed out, and she scoffed.

"Maybe someday. Here's what I do know. When you're ready for it to happen, it will. When you're both tired of maintaining two apartments when you're always only at one, it will happen. When you both decide you can trust each other with your heart forever, it will happen. Don't rush it or give it an unnecessary timeline, okay? That's going to be a recipe for disaster. Look what happened with the whole *I'm going to be dating someone seriously by my birthday* fiasco."

I held up my finger and lowered my brow toward my nose. "But, I am seriously dating someone."

Amber chuckled and shook her head at me as she walked toward the front of the bakery for the banner. "You are, but you sure kissed a lot of frogs to get there. Imagine if you'd just seen what was right in front of your eyes."

155

She disappeared into the front, but her words stayed with me while I packed and prepped for the competition. Imagine if I'd just seen what was right in front of my eyes.

I imagine I would have had to kiss a lot fewer frogs to find my prince.

The weather was less than ideal for topping cupcakes with buttercream icing. It was over eighty inside the building, even with the industrial fans running, and besides me being hot and sweaty, my frosting was going to be drooping and falling off if I didn't figure something out fast. Brady had already filled the berries with cream cheese and dipped them in chocolate, leaving them in the small fridge to harden. I didn't want to put the cupcakes in the refrigerator, though. That would make them cold and hard for the judges rather than fluffy and light as they were meant to be.

"Do we have any parchment paper left?" I asked Brady, sweat on my brow that I swiped away with my sleeve.

"About the size of a piece of toilet paper," he joked, pulling it out and setting it down.

"That will work. I need a small pan that will fit in the fridge."

His brow went down, but he grabbed the lid from a CamSquare and set it down. "Will that work?"

"Perfectly."

I covered it with the minuscule piece of parchment paper and piped on three plumes of icing, immediately sticking it in the fridge to harden. Brady's eyes smiled as he prepped the cupcakes, having filled them with our strawberry cream cheese center and plated them to await the final touches.

I started to clean up the workspace and kept my eye on Darla. She was dressed to the nines in a summer sundress meant for the beach and not a bake-off, complete with matching heels and a flower crown. She looked ridiculous, but maybe that was just because I hate her.

I eyed her again.

No, she looked ridiculous.

I enjoyed the fact that she was sweating up a storm, and the back of her dress was soaking wet as she labored to finish her three cupcakes in time. There were five minutes left on the clock, and I was done other than hardening the icing, which wouldn't take long in the deep cold. The icing only had to last until they got into the judges' hands. After that, they'd be eaten too fast for them to care. Darla, on the other hand, wasn't having that kind of luck. Her frosting was runny like water rather than holding any sort of shape. I should be a nice person and tell her how to fix it, but I'm not a nice person when it comes to Darla. Besides, with less than five minutes to go, there wasn't time for her to correct her tactical error now.

Unfortunately, Team Barton had dropped out of the competition at noon. The better half of Team Barton had gone into labor with their second child most unexpectedly. She was whisked away by ambulance to the hospital, and we were waiting for word on the outcome. Lila was a few weeks away from her due date and thought she'd make it through the bake-off easily, but this heat, and the baby, had different ideas. That left just us and Darla to fight to the end for the best cupcake of the year. But it looked like Darla brought her F game to the table.

Checking the clock, I had three minutes to go. I piped a small amount of icing on each cupcake for the cold plumes to adhere to and grabbed them from the cooler. After adding the frosting to each cupcake, Brady garnished them with a stuffed strawberry and hit our timer. We were done with two minutes to spare, and Brady carried the plate of cupcakes to the judges to present them. While Darla squirted and spread, huffed and moaned, I stared her down, hoping to unnerve her. It wasn't the mature thing to do, but after she tried to rip my hair out, I didn't much care about what was mature.

She tossed the frosting bag down with a bang, plated the cupcakes, and hit her timer with twenty seconds left to go. After dropping them at the judges' table, she hurried back to hers to start her clean up. She had to be ready to run to the pageant building when the judges finished declaring the winner. Something told me she already knew it wasn't going to be her. Her cupcakes were probably edible, but the icing was a gloppy mess that looked like she had barely mixed the milk and powdered sugar before plopping it on.

"I think Darla bit off more than she could chew this year," Brady said from the side of his lip while we stood in front of our tables. We had to wait for the judges to leave the tent before we could do the same.

"In her case, I hope she chokes on it," I said quietly just as Mr. Samson grabbed the microphone.

"Okay, everyone. We will take a thirty-minute break to judge the cupcakes. Normally, we'd give you an hour, but since we are down one team, it won't take as long. Please be back here at three for our announcement."

They left the stage area, and the audience also dispersed to get refreshments and some fresh air. It was stifling in the building, and I was going to be glad when we could clean up and head over to where Amber was waiting to taste test the new cupcakes. We planned it for three-thirty, but I was happy to have the extra half an hour between jobs. At least the tent Amber was in had more airflow and better fans.

Brady's phone rang, and he glanced at the number, his brow going down. "I should take this," he said, and I motioned him out of the tent.

"Go ahead. I'll start cleaning up."

He jogged away with his phone to his ear, and I worked on the rest of the clean-up. Since we work as a team, we do the majority of our clean-up as we go. I refused to wash all of my tools in the minuscule sink we had to share with Darla, though, so I'd take them back to the bakery to clean them. Besides, I was not about to deal with Darla when Brady wasn't around. Thankfully, she didn't notice that he'd left. She was concentrating on finishing her work, so she could move on to be the next big thing as a beauty queen. I had to fight to keep from rolling my eyes on the off-chance Darla noticed.

I grabbed my phone, checking the time. It had been ten minutes since Brady left, but it was a Friday, so a vendor might have had a question about our order. I sent Amber a text and let her know we were ahead of schedule and would be there sooner than three-thirty to help her with the cupcakes. All I had left to do was grab a drink of water and wait for the judges to make their decision. I was looking forward to six o'clock tonight when I could go home, take a shower, and fall into bed. My exhaustion was another reason I was ready to be done with this bake-off every year.

Okay, so if we slept instead of making love all night, I might not be as tired as I am right now, but let's not get crazy. Besides, I've been exhausted for months. Keeping up the pace at the bakery as the business grew was taking a lot out of me. I didn't need competitions like this one to get customers now. Thankfully, Brady agreed with me when I talked to him about it on the way over. He was more than happy to take an afternoon to enjoy Strawberry Fest with me and not have to worry about the work involved with the competition. We'd still have our booth, that's just good business, but we'd be able to spell Amber if we weren't tied up here, which was a bonus.

My phone dinged with a text from Amber, telling me she was more than ready to reveal the cupcakes as people were already waiting. I promised to text her the second I knew who won. If it was us, she could break them out before we got there rather than wait. My eyes drifted to the clock on my phone, and it had been fifteen minutes since Brady left. I pushed the cart filled with our supplies to the door and left it on the square marked for Team Fluffy

Cupcake, then ducked out of the building to breathe air that wasn't quite as hot as inside. I searched for Brady, wondering if he'd decided to run to the bathroom before he came back. I had better text him and let him know he was going to be late. Both members of the team had to be present when the judges returned with the results.

I sent him a quick text saying he better get back inside, then headed to the table to wait for him and the judges. I was glad that Darla was off at the sink cleaning her dishes frantically, so she could get out of the building as soon as the judges announced a winner. She was soaking wet, her hair was a disheveled mess under her flower crown, and her makeup was smeared from wiping her face. Only an amateur wears make-up to a baking competition in the middle of July, I thought, rolling my eyes.

Brady strode back into the tent, and my heart went pitter-patter, my stomach swooping when I gazed into his handsome face. I was head over heels in love with this man. Maybe the swooping was fear that I was going to lose him when the newness of the relationship wore off, and he realized I had so many issues he'd have to deal with from my past. Then again, most of those issues had disappeared since Brady had been the one loving me every night.

He put his arm around my waist and his lips near my ear. "I have great news!"

At that moment, the judges filed back into the room, and Mr. Samson grabbed the microphone. "We have reached a decision. Is everyone here?"

Darla was standing at her table the same as we were, and most of the spectators were back in their seats.

"We're all here," I said, wishing I had time to hear Brady's news, but I didn't want to look rude in front of the judges either.

"Then, without further ado, let's announce our winner! Both cupcakes were light, airy, and perfectly baked. However, the icing on Berry Sinful was quite delightful. We believe the secret ingredient was marshmallow fluff?" he asked, and I gave the nod. All three judges did a fist pump at their cupcake eating prowess. "We thought so! The combination with the strawberries and cream cheese was perfectly sinful for sure. Therefore, Berry Sinful has won the title at Strawberry Fest Bake-off this year! Congratulations, Team Fluffy Cupcake, for a fine performance, and thank you, Darla, for the wonderful runner-up cupcake."

Mr. Samson put the microphone down and carried the trophy to us, his smile wide as he passed it over for us to admire. We smiled happily for the camera while we took pictures with the judges and at our tables. Thankfully, Darla remained at her table when they took the full shot.

After the pictures were taken and the congratulations were over, I addressed the spectators. "Amber is at our booth in the food tent. If you want to head over, she has samples of Berry Sinful ready for you to enjoy. Thanks for being here today and supporting Strawberry Fest and our business."

The mass exodus from the building had me grabbing my phone and sending Amber a picture of the trophy and the words, *get ready*. I chuckled to myself and put the phone down, turning to Brady to hear his news when Darla interrupted us.

"Well, if it isn't fatso and her adorable BF. What's that old poem? Jack Sprat could eat no fat. His wife could eat no lean. You two personify that like no one else I've ever known."

Brady stepped in front of me and leaned on the table. "Do you have a point, Darla?"

"No, she doesn't," I said, stepping to the side, so we looked like a team rather than him as my protector. "She has sour grapes because her frosting looked like bird crap, and ours was quite delightful."

If steam really could pour from someone's ears, Darla's could be powering a locomotive.

"It isn't even fair that you're in this competition," she growled. "Professionals shouldn't be allowed to compete!"

"I'll make sure to tell the judges to change the bylaws," I drawled dryly.

"Is there anything else we can do for you, Darla? I think you better run along to the makeup and hair tent. You are a bit of a mess, and that crown is waiting. Better use your extra time to perfect your beauty queen look," Brady said cheerily.

"I plan on it. I also plan to win. It's a shame you decided to date this fat bitch instead of me. You deserve so much better than her. You could be fucking a beauty queen every night. Instead, you're fucking the town's orphan no one wanted. How does it feel to be the pity fuck, fluffy?" she asked before she spun on her heel and flounced away.

Refusing to react and let her see how much that hurt, I kept a smile glued to my face until she left the building, her tight ass swaying as she pranced away on those heels like the true bitch that she is.

"Haylee," he said, but I held up my hand, taking a deep breath, so my actual reaction to her words didn't run down my cheeks.

"Just—it's fine. We need to pack this stuff in the van and get over to the tent before Amber is overrun by cupcake eaters."

"Not until I make myself clear," he growled. "You are not, nor will you ever be, unwanted or a pity fuck," he said, pointing to where Darla had stood. "Do you understand me?"

"She's not wrong in her assessment, though, Brady. Maybe not about the pity fuck, but about being the town's orphan. I'm almost thirty, and if I count the people who care about me, I can use one hand and have fingers left over." I waved my hand. "Forget it. We need to go," I said, grabbing the handle of the cart and pushing it out into the air.

It had cooled off, and clouds were building in the sky, leaving a hazy cast to the afternoon that meant storms were coming. With any luck, we'd get the cupcake tasting done and the booth packed up before the rain hit.

"I'm going to move the van over by the tent," I said to him over my shoulder. "If it starts to rain, we can't be transporting product that far. Why don't you head to the food tent and help Amber until I get there?"

He grasped the cart and pulled it to a stop. "I'll load this and move the van. You're the cupcake baker and should be there first. Let me do the heavy lifting for the rest of the day."

"Sure. Okay," I said, releasing the cart. "Just don't be too long. Storms are coming, and it's not safe to be in a tent."

"You'll see me in ten," he promised. "And Haylee," he said, his brow down to his nose, "I love you, more than anything. More than the love of one thousand friends. Okay?"

I nodded, trying for a smile but barely getting a trembling lip tilt. "I love you, too."

He leaned over for a gentle kiss to seal his words and then pushed the cart toward the parking lot while I diverted to the tent.

I did love him, but unfortunately, Darla was right. He deserved better.

Twenty-One

The food tent was packed when I arrived, and most of the cupcakes had already fled the scene. Amber had given me a look that could mean nothing other than *help me!* I waded right in, helping her hand out samples of the cupcakes, accept congratulations on another winning entry, and take cash from people's hands as they snatched up prepackaged cupcakes like sugar addicts looking for a fix. I wasn't complaining. The more they bought, the less we had to pack up and take back to the bakery when it was time to go home.

It had been almost thirty minutes when I realized I hadn't seen Brady yet. "Hey, Amber," I said, now that the crowd was down to a manageable size. "Have you seen Brady around anywhere? He was supposed to bring the van over here half an hour ago."

"He came in about ten minutes ago and gave me the van keys. Then his phone rang, so he stepped out. It was way too loud in here," she answered. A rumble of thunder boomed in the distance, and she grimaced, turning her head toward the door of the tent. "We're almost out of cupcakes and bread. I think we need to pack up and get out of here."

When Amber was thirteen, she'd been caught in a tornado in the family camper. It roared through the campground while they were sleeping, and she barely survived. She still lives with the after-effects of it now with her leg. She also has severe PTSD about thunderstorms, which is to be expected, and this storm was taking us by surprise.

"I agree. I'll take the product to the van while you take down the banners and grab the rest. Leave the tables and chairs. They will break them down tomorrow."

She handed me the key to the van, and I gathered the few containers of cupcakes and loaves of bread we had left, stacking them on the cart. I grabbed the cash box, too, and then pushed the cart toward the van. Once I had this stowed away, I'd look for Brady and let him know it was time to go.

When I finished loading the van, I still didn't see him anywhere. I leaned on the back of the bumper to wait for Amber to bring the rest of the supplies and decided to text him. It was going to rain, and we needed to get out of here sooner rather than later if we were going to get the truck unloaded before it stormed. Then, I heard his laughter near the front of the tent. I peeked around the door, and he was talking to one of the Strawberry Fest committee members.

"No, we aren't a thing," I heard him say. "We went out for a few weeks, but she's too needy and emotional."

"Really?" the committee member asked. "That surprises me. She's always so put together and confident."

"It's an act," Brady said, his head shaking. "She has no self-confidence, and her self-esteem is equally nonexistent. I've come to realize I can't be with a woman like that."

The committee member said something else, but I didn't hear it over the roaring in my ears. Was he talking about me? Brady's phone rang again, and he told Mr. Cavanaugh goodbye and then answered the call. I ducked back behind the door, so he didn't see me. He had to be talking about me, right? He hasn't dated anyone else for a few weeks at a time, at least that's what he told me that night in my apartment. The night I let him into my bed and my heart. Why would Brady say something like that to someone he hardly knew, though, when he had just told me he loved me. He just asked me to be his girlfriend last night, and now he's claiming he can't be with a woman like me?

The truth dawned, and I swallowed back the bile. Maybe Brady was embarrassed for people to know we were together. Wait. That doesn't make any sense either. Sure, we work together, but he asked me to be his girlfriend. How did he think he was going to hide that from people?

"Thank you, Baker Robinson," I heard Brady say, laughter in his voice again. "I guess you heard the news already." There was a pause, and then Brady chuckled. "I'm highly sought after now. I didn't even know my application had been approved. I've already had two job offers come into my email since this morning. Wait, what?" he asked, his voice pausing again. "You want me to take over your bakery?" He paused again, and I swallowed back the tears gathering in my eyes. Was he going to leave The Fluffy Cupcake? Was he applying to other bakeries? Why didn't he tell me? What the hell was going on?

I couldn't decide if I should be hurt or angry, but either way, he had to know I wasn't leaving my business here in Lake Pendle, right? He asks me to be his girlfriend and then starts applying to other places? Maybe he thinks it will be too awkward to work for me now that we're dating each other, but I warned him about that. He said he had no problem keeping the two separate, and so far, he hadn't. Besides, if he were just going to work at a different bakery, he wouldn't be talking to his old boss from Milwaukee.

Amber dumped everything in the back of the van with her eye on the sky. I slammed the doors, not even caring if Brady heard me, and motioned to the front of the van, praying my voice didn't wobble when I spoke. "I'm going to take the truck back to the bakery and get it unloaded before the storms roll in."

"What about Brady?" she asked, as more thunder rumbled in the distance.

Cupcake

"Give him a ride home for me? Tell him I'll talk to him later," I said, jumping into the cargo van and trying to close the door.

She grabbed the handle before I could slam it and pinned me with a look. "What's going on, Haylee. You can't just leave him here."

"I'm not," I said, gritting my teeth to keep the tears at bay. "You're here and can give him a ride in your car. I'm sure he'll be done with his call soon. Just let him know when you're ready to leave. I'll see you tomorrow."

"I think you should wait for him. He won't be happy if you don't," she said, still holding onto the door.

"I don't care if he's happy or not," I said, relieved when she released the handle. "I'll see you tomorrow."

I started the van and pulled away, refusing to look in the mirror to see the look of shock on Amber's face or the tears on mine.

Something was going on with Haylee, and I had no idea what it was. I checked the clock again, and it was after eight o'clock in the morning. The Fluffy Cupcake was still without its main cupcake. I knew she was upstairs, but she refused to answer the door when I knocked. I even sent Amber up to talk to her, but she wouldn't answer the door for her, either.

When I finished my call yesterday, the bakery van was gone, and so was she. Amber gave me a ride back to the bakery to grab my car, and the van was in its usual spot. Haylee's car wasn't next to it like it should have been, though. I didn't know where she'd gone, but she wouldn't answer my texts or calls. I figured it had something to do with what Darla had said at the competition. I thought I'd taken care of that situation, but clearly, I was mistaken.

I untied my apron and hung it on the hook, stopping in the doorway of the bakery until Amber's customer left and closed the door behind her. "Something is wrong," I said, my shoulders slumping. "Very wrong."

"I agree," she said, handing me a cup of coffee. "She never goes incognito for this long, and she always shows up to do her baking. I know we have extra product made, but it's the weekend, and there are special orders to do. I don't understand what's going on. Maybe she's sick and plans to come in later to get the orders done for tomorrow?"

I lowered myself to a chair and sipped the coffee. "I think Darla really got to her yesterday. She was cruel, Amber. Beyond anything you've ever heard."

"She was mad that she lost, right?" she asked, rolling her eyes. "She's that way every year."

"She wasn't happy about losing the competition, no. She said professionals shouldn't be allowed to compete. If it had only been that, Haylee would have brushed it off. But Darla quoted the nursery rhyme Jack Sprat."

"Fuck," Amber said, drawing out the last syllable. "Pardon my French, but I know that didn't go over well."

"I think she would have ignored her if Darla hadn't then called her the town orphan no one wanted to be followed immediately by saying she was a pity fuck."

"Oh my God," Amber sighed, dropping her chin to her chest. "This is bad, Brady. Nothing gets to her more than being reminded that her parents didn't want her."

"I know. After Darla left, Haylee said she could count how many people love her on one hand with fingers left over. I want to give her space, and I know I should, but I'm afraid of what she'll do if she gets too bogged down in what someone as insignificant as Darla thinks or says."

Amber nodded. "I agree. Once Taylor gets here, I'll use my spare key to her apartment and go in."

"I'm done with the baking," I said, standing immediately. "Give me the key, and I'll go."

She swung her head a hair and pursed her lips. "I think you should let me, Brady. This situation feels like a two-part process. She needs to cry on my shoulder about it first before she'll be able to hear what you have to say."

I tossed up my hand and let it fall to my side. "My voice should be the loudest voice Haylee hears!" I exclaimed, angry that Haylee wouldn't talk to me.

Amber held out her hands to calm me. "It should be, but Brady, being in a relationship is new to her, and the things Darla said, they implied she doesn't deserve that relationship, right?"

I nodded, some of the anger draining away. "She said I could be dating and fucking a beauty queen every night instead of dating the fatso no one wanted."

Amber leaned on the counter and sucked in air deeply, her eyes flashing with anger. "Darla so needs to disappear from this town," she ground out.

"Don't let anyone hear you say that," I warned, just in case she had plans to make it happen.

"I meant to find a new city, Brady." She shook her head. "I'm so tired of the way she poisons this town."

"There's always one in every town, I've learned. Eventually, something will happen to put Darla in her place. When it does, things might change. For now, we have to take care of our cupcake."

"And you have to trust that I know the best way to do that."

I held up my hand. "Okay, you're right. There is so much history between Haylee and Darla, and you and Haylee. I just want to be the one she runs to when she's scared, not away from."

"Did you do anything to upset her?" she asked, her head cocked to the side.

I held my hands up against my chest. "Not that I'm aware of, no. I didn't even get a chance to tell her that I passed my master baker exam and am officially certified. They called me while we were waiting for the judging. By the time I got back into the building, the judges were back with their decision."

"Brady!" she exclaimed, running around the counter to hug me. "Congratulations! That's a major accomplishment! I remember when Hay-Hay finally got hers. It's like getting a master's degree after years of hard work."

I patted her back before I released her. "Thank you. It is exciting. It would be more exciting if I weren't worried about Haylee, but you're right. It takes four years of hard work even to apply to take the test, so finally getting the accreditation feels wonderful."

"Why don't you go home and take a nap? I'll call you once I talk to Hay-Hay."

I shook my head, my earlier fatigue vanquished by the coffee and knowing Amber had my back with our girl. "I know I'm not the lead cupcake baker here, but I can hold my own when it comes to making and decorating them. I'm going to get her special orders done for tomorrow, so she can breathe when she comes in tonight. If she comes in tonight," I added, biting my lip.

"She will," Amber said with confidence. "This is her business, and she won't neglect it for long. I can promise you that she knows exactly what she has to do and how long it will take her. If you want to do it, though, I won't stop you. Besides, it will show her that you're her partner in the relationship and the bakery. Sometimes seeing someone's thoughtfulness for where you are in life says more than any words can."

I pointed at her and winked. "Exactly what I was thinking. You know where I am if you need me."

I headed straight to the cooler to get the first batch of cupcakes that were already made but not yet decorated. I would work all day and night again if it meant Haylee trusted me to have her back in life.

Twenty-Two

I took a deep breath before I knocked on the office door in the 4-H building. It was only eight a.m., and I should be at the bakery, but there was something I needed to do before the parade started at noon. If I were smart, I'd turn around and pretend I didn't know this information, but I couldn't with a good conscience. The town of Lake Pendle deserved to know the truth.

"Come in," called a voice from the other side of the door.

I pushed it open, and Mrs. Mulberry sat at the makeshift desk with piles of paperwork and ribbons around her.

"Hi, Mrs. Mulberry," I said, scooting sideways to fit into the small office. "I hope I'm not interrupting."

She motioned around and chuckled. "Hi, Haylee. I'm just working on the usual stuff that has to get done before the parade. I'm secretly glad today is the last day of the fair. I'm exhausted, but it sure was well attended this year, wasn't it?"

I nodded my agreement. The older woman was echoing what I was feeling about it, too. "It grows every year, which is wonderful to see."

"Did you hear the good news?" she asked, standing up to join me by the door. "Mrs. Barton had a baby boy last night at six o'clock. Phillip John Barton was six pounds and healthy as a horse. Probably all those cupcakes," she said with a wink.

I chuckled and gave her a little shoulder bump. "That's wonderful news. We were worried when we hadn't heard anything when we left last night. I'm so glad everything turned out well for them."

"Was this a social visit, dear, or did you need something?" she asked right before she snapped her fingers. "I bet you're here for your sticker, aren't you? Oh dear, I wonder where that is," she said, tapping her chin.

I waved my hand immediately. "No, the committee always delivers it once everything is ready. Don't worry about it, please. I'm here about a different matter. Well, two, actually."

"Oh, well, hopefully, I can help," she said, "I don't have much time."

"I know, that's why I'm here early. I wanted to let you know that we won't be competing in any further cupcake competitions as a bakery. I think after all these years, I can no longer consider myself anything but a professional, and that's not fair to the other teams who want to compete."

"Hmmm," she hummed, her lips in a frown. "I suppose you are right in that matter. There is no rule about it, though."

"I know there isn't, and the committee should probably consider changing that. If they do, they could even consider doing a bake-off between bakeries or something that gives the professionals a handicap. The bragging rights are fun and all, but I feel like when others know they're going up against professional bakers, they won't even bother to sign up. Does that make sense?"

"It does," she agreed. "I'll bring it to the rest of the committee to consider before next year."

"Great. Let me know if I can help with judging or for ideas on ways to get the professionals involved but still keep the competition clean for the amateurs. I knew it was time to stop competing when I decided to give the trophy to the second-place winner if we won again this year. It no longer felt right to keep it."

"Oh, should I have the sticker go to Darla then?" she asked, her head tipped to the side.

"No. I didn't give it to Darla. I will be giving the trophy to the Bartons, though. It can be a fun story they tell little Phillip when he's old enough."

"Whatever you'd like to do, dear," she said with confusion.

"Darla is the second reason I'm here," I said, swallowing down the panic, so my voice stayed even.

"I know you two have never gotten along," she agreed. "Did something happen?"

"You could say that, on both accounts," I agreed. "I don't know where her issues with me come from, truthfully."

"Darla is just that way, Haylee. She picks the person she thinks is the weakest and uses them to make herself look better."

"That's what Brady said, too," I whispered, doubt creeping in about what I thought I knew about Brady Pearson. "Regardless, I heard she won Strawberry Fest Princess last night."

"Fair and square," she said. "We brought in judges from outside of the county, so there was no favoritism."

"That was a good idea," I said, pulling my phone from my pocket. "The thing is, I don't know if you want someone like Darla representing the city as the princess. I didn't know it yesterday when she approached us after the competition, but my recording app was still open on my phone. I always record the judges' decision and use the sound bites for advertising and such," I explained, nervously swallowing around the lump in my throat. "I was playing it back last night and was surprised to hear that it had also captured an exchange between us that occurred after the judging. Can I play it for you? Fair warning, some of her language is colorful."

She motioned for me to go ahead, so I hit the play button, the audio already cued up to play at the right spot. I let the whole thing play, even the part where I got snippy with her. I believed I was justified in what I said, but even if

173

Mrs. Mulberry didn't, she would have to agree Darla started the whole thing.

When I clicked the phone off, she stood in disbelief, her mouth hanging open. "She just started that out of the blue?"

I shrugged callously. "Not exactly out of the blue. She lost the bake-off and wasn't happy about it. I probably shouldn't have egged her on, but she could have walked away. That's not taking into account what happened at the bakery a few weeks ago." I explained to her about the fight and how I refused to press charges as long as she stayed away.

"This isn't good," she fretted. "I wish we had known about that. We don't allow anyone to participate in the pageant if they aren't upstanding members of the community. They have to be good ambassadors. We all know she can be snippy, but I didn't know there was this kind of thing going on in the background."

"She likes it that way," I said, everything weighing heavily on my shoulders now. "The more people she fools, the more she can get away with."

"I need to call the other committee members. I don't know what to do. Is there a way to get me a copy of that?" she asked, pointing at the phone.

Anticipating that request, I had made an MP3 of it before I left home. "I can email it to the email address I have for the committee if that helps."

She patted my shoulder with her lips turned down in a frown. "That would help. I'm going to call everyone now."

I attached the file to an email and sent it, holding it up for her to see. "I put in the body that you'd be calling everyone. I'll let you go. Thanks for listening to what I had to say. I just thought you should know."

She patted my shoulder on her way to the desk to make her calls. "Thank you for bringing it to our attention. I'll let you know what our decision is."

I stopped in the doorway and gave her a sad smile. "Either way, I don't feel good about this, Mrs. Mulberry, so just do what you think is best for the festival and the town.

Enjoy the rest of the fair," I said, tapping the doorframe and heading back to my car.

What I said was the truth. I didn't feel good about what I'd just done, but I also couldn't give Darla another pass. She'd gotten nothing but passes for her entire life from the time she was a little girl. It was time for her to own up to her decisions in life. She needed to know her words would come back to haunt her.

I sat down in my car, the weight of the world heavy, and rested my head on the headrest. Something told me if the committee pulled her crown, I'd hear about it sooner rather than later, but what was done was done. I started the car and pulled out of the parking spot and back toward the bakery, knowing I needed to face my responsibilities there, too. When I parked next to my apartment and noticed Brady's car was still on the street, I decided those responsibilities could wait until he was gone.

I quickly jogged up the stairs, so no one saw me, and locked the door. Just the thought of Brady's conversations that I overheard at the fair made pain and anguish stab through my heart like a hot poker. There was no way I could work with him and pretend everything was okay.

I sank onto the couch and buried my face in my hands, the tears falling again. I'd cried so many tears since yesterday afternoon I didn't think I had any left to cry. How could I be so naïve? Darla was right. There was no reason for Brady to be with me. If nothing else, shirking my duties at the bakery would prove it to him. Maybe then he would take that job in Milwaukee and leave me and my business far behind. Brady deserved to run a bakery. He deserved to be with someone who had fewer issues than I did, too. Someone with a family behind them that he could call his own eventually. I didn't have that, and now, I never would.

"It's time to face your fears, Haylee," I said to the woman staring back at me in the mirror.

I shut off the bathroom light and walked to the front door, somewhat ashamed of my behavior in the last thirty-six hours, but also proud I had stood up for myself against Darla. I hadn't heard anything from the committee, which meant they hadn't done anything about it. That was okay. My conscience was clear. I'd done what I could to make it known the kind of person she was behind the community's back. It still stymied me that she had lived here all these years and had managed to fool everyone with her lies. She wasn't fooling me. With any luck, she wasn't fooling the members of the committee anymore, either.

That was then, and this is now. At almost midnight, I had to get downstairs and start baking. I had three hours until Brady would show up, and I planned to be done with everything at the bench, so I could be at the decorating table while he was making bread. We'd have to talk, but I couldn't do it during work hours. I had planned to go in after he left yesterday, but I was too exhausted to remember my name. I hadn't slept the night before, and there was no way I was going to be able to hold it together long enough to work around dangerous equipment.

I'd texted Amber and told her I was sick and was going to bed. I promised her I'd be in at midnight to get the baking done, and she'd texted me back saying she understood. I half expected her to show up early to talk to me since she'd been trying since we left the fair on Friday night. I felt shitty about it, but sometimes, a girl just needed to sulk.

I grabbed my keys and opened the door, locking it behind me and tucking my keys in my pocket. I was halfway down the stairs when a shadow stepped away from the side of the building.

"It's about time, bitch," she said, her words slurring slightly.

I froze, surprised to see Darla climbing the steps below me. "What do you want, Darla?" I asked nervously. "I need to start baking."

"What do I want?" she asked, spittle flying toward me. If her words were poison, I'd be dead. "I want to know why you were secretly recording me! And then to go to the festival committee to nark on me. Bad move, bitch."

"I wasn't secretly recording you," I assured her, tired of her vendetta against me. "I always record the competition. I didn't know my phone was still recording when you came over to us. Lucky for me, but not so lucky for you. Now they know you're a bitch. Then again, that's not big news," I said, giving her a shrug.

Before I could brace for it, her arm darted out, and she slapped me across the face. "Watch your tone, fatso," she spat, having to right herself from the momentum of the slap. She was drunk. I could smell it on her breath every time she opened her mouth. My cheek stung, but it wasn't enough to give her the satisfaction of rubbing it. I did need to deescalate the situation and get away from her before she did something worse than slap me.

"Listen, Darla, I need to get to work. If you'll excuse me," I said, trying to slide down to the next step to break away from her.

"There is no excuse for you," she hissed, her face right up in mine in a way that could only be construed as threatening. The smell of vodka on her fetid breath made me want to gag, but I resisted, afraid that would set her off. "They took my crown from me as I was getting on the float. Do you know how humiliating that was?" she asked, her voice going up several octaves as she encroached on my space more.

"I'm sorry, Darla. That wasn't my intention," I said calmly.

She laughed, but the sound was nothing but evil. "Oh, sure. The poor pitiful bitch who had her feelings hurt didn't mean to start trouble. You've always acted the victim to get what you want. The game is old now, and you really should get new material."

"*I've* always acted the victim? Seriously?" I asked in astonishment. "You're the one who has spent twenty-five years bullying me, Darla. I don't know what I ever did to you to deserve it. Regardless, I'm done now. You can be you, and I can be me. As long as you don't step foot on my property again, we'll get along just fine. Now, if you'll excuse me, I have a bakery to run."

Her growl froze me in my tracks. "There you go again, rubbing in how successful you are because you run a bakery. I can make you unsuccessful in less than two seconds," she said, her eyes wild and crazy. They were the last thing I saw before I was lying on my back, staring up at the sky filled with bright, twinkling stars.

"How do you like me now, bitch?" she asked, spitting in my face.

I tried to get up, but I couldn't make my limbs move when I gave them the order. I couldn't get words to come out of my mouth, either. Darla was starting to swim above me like a freaky monster from a horror film. It struck me that I was going to die here without telling Brady I was sorry.

"Are you out of words?" she asked, giving me a kick with the toe of her sandal. It dug into my hip, and I grunted, the pain flaring to life in every part of me. The only satisfaction I got was the motion made her tip to the side where she fell to her hands and knees on the ground.

When she stood back up, she took two steps to the left before she steadied herself. "Here comes the fun part," she said, her hand reaching for something in her pocket as the stars dimmed, and the roaring in my ears gave way to silence.

Twenty-Three

I parked my car on the street, surprised that there were still no lights on in the bakery. Amber had texted me that Haylee was going to start baking at midnight, so I texted back that I was going to get here early to talk to her. It took some convincing, but she finally relented and agreed to let me try talking to her first before she stepped in. I knew Haylee was upset about Darla, but something told me there was more to it. She was scared of what was happening between us. The only person who could reassure her about that was me.

I checked the clock, and it was only a little after twelve. Maybe Haylee overslept, so I decided to head up to the apartment and pound on the door until she opened it. Anxiety filled my stomach with dread at the darkness around the building at this time of night. I always hated the lack of lighting at the back, but Haylee refused to put in motion sensor lights. She said it was unnecessary in a town like Lake Pendle. Maybe she was right, but the small light over the bakery door barely offered any light for her to walk up and down from her apartment.

I tripped on something lying on the ground by the steps and fell to my knee. "What the hell?" I asked until my eyes landed on the prone form by my leg. My breath caught, and my heart pounded in my chest as I gazed at the woman I love. She was out cold.

179

"Haylee," I yelled frantically, slapping her cheek gently in hopes she'd come around. "Haylee, sweetheart, come on," I said, my hand going to her neck to check for a pulse. She was breathing, and her pulse was steady, but she wasn't responding.

I grabbed my phone and dialed 911, waiting impatiently for the call to be answered.

"911. What's your emergency?" the operator asked.

"My girlfriend, she's hurt. I think she fell down the stairs."

"Where are you, sir?" she asked, her tone bored as she typed away on the computer keyboard.

"Behind The Fluffy Cupcake," I said. "Uhh…the address is…dammit! What's the address?"

"Is this Brady?" the woman asked.

"Yes!" I exclaimed, "yes, it's me, Brady Pearson."

"This is Lynn Fleming. I've got a rig dispatched. Who is the victim, and what are her injuries?"

"It's Haylee!" I exclaimed, my throat closing in on the words. My hand was wet when I pulled it away from her neck, and the red stain made my heart pound in my chest. "Oh God, she's bleeding and unconscious," I said, my tone of voice telling her more than my words. I was scared that I was watching the woman I love die. "I don't know what happened."

"Hang on, Brady," she said as she typed. "I need to let the EMTs know the specifics."

"Should I check her for injuries?"

"No!" she exclaimed. "Don't move her if you don't have to. She could have hurt her neck if she fell."

I held the phone under my chin and rubbed Haylee's face tenderly with my thumbs, whispering to her without moving her head. She moaned, and her lids fluttered.

"She's coming around," I said to the operator.

"Do you hear the sirens?"

"Yes," I said, letting out the breath I'd been holding.

"Good. Don't move her. Keep her still until they arrive."

"I will. Thank you!" I exclaimed, hitting the off button and sticking it in my pocket.

I held her face gently, so she didn't move her neck as she started to come around. "Hey, sweetheart," I said tenderly. "The ambulance is almost here. They're going to take you to the hospital and check you out."

"Brady?" she asked, her voice low and whispery.

"Yes, it's me. I found you here at the bottom of the stairs. You're okay now," I promised, even though I was worried she was far from okay. I didn't want to check her over and risk her moving her head. "What happened, cupcake?"

She blinked a couple of times and swallowed, grimacing when I wouldn't let her move. "Let me sit up."

I shook my head as the sirens screamed closer. "No can do, pretty lady. The 911 operator said to keep you still until the EMTs arrive. They're almost here. Did you fall?"

"Pushed," she said, coughing once and then grimacing again.

"You were pushed down the stairs?" I asked, stymied by what she was saying. Who would push her down the stairs?

"Halfway down," she said, swallowing around the dryness in her throat to answer me. "She was waiting for me."

"She who?" I asked as the ambulance pulled to the curb, and the flashing lights lit up the scene better.

"Darla," she croaked. "Weapon."

The EMTs ran up to us and dropped their bags. "Thank God, she's awake," the woman said as she knelt next to Haylee. "It's me, Haylee," she said, sliding a neck brace around her neck so I could stand back.

"Kanee?" Haylee asked as the other EMT readied an I.V.

"Yup, and I'm with that loser that you know as Liam."

Haylee chuckled but then grimaced as I knelt by her forehead, stroking her long hair back out of her face. "Do you know them?"

"Went to school with them," she croaked. "Kanee loves black forest, and Liam is a straight-up vanilla kind of guy."

"Hey," he said, chuckling as he checked her for injuries. "I'm not that vanilla. I'll h—" He stopped short and glanced up at Kanee. "We need to move her. Now."

"What's the matter?" I asked, glancing between them.

"Knife wound," he said, pointing at the spot near her shoulder that had now bled through her white chef coat, turning it a crimson red. I hadn't seen it until the ambulance lights illuminated her better.

"Does anything else hurt, Haylee?" Kanee asked, grabbing the backboard from Liam.

"My arm," she said right away, "and my head. My head feels like it's stuffed with gauze."

"We need to get you to the hospital, okay? Liam is going to roll you forward, and I'm going to get the board under you. Don't try to help. Let us do the work." Kanee looked up at me. "Hold her head, so it rolls with us. Can you do that?"

I nodded and helped them roll her, her moan loud as another car pulled up on the scene. I was worried it was Amber, so I was relieved when Officer Stevens jogged over. "Haylee!" he exclaimed as they carried her to the rig and got her situated on the stretcher. "I heard it on the scanner and had to check it out. What the hell happened?"

I held up my finger to him and stood next to the stretcher. "I'm going to talk to Officer Stevens, and then I'll be right behind you. You do what the EMTs tell you, okay? I love you."

Her eyes were already closed, and I don't know if she heard me since they'd already given her something through her I.V., but I had to hope she had. Kanee pushed her into the rig and stuck her head out the door.

"We'll see you at Mauston Memorial?" she asked, and I nodded.

"Give me five minutes with Stevens, and I'll be there."

She shut the door, and the rig pulled away, the lights and sirens blaring.

"I'll give you a ride over," he shouted, pointing at his car.

I buckled in and leaned my head back on the seat, my hands shaking and covered in her blood. "She was going to work," I said as he pulled away from the curb, his lights going, but sirens quiet. "I decided I'd see if she needed any help after the long weekend and found her there. Thank God I decided not to wait until three a.m."

He grasped my shoulder and squeezed. "Take a deep breath, Brady. Did she say what happened?"

I sucked in air and held it, letting it out before I spoke. "She said Darla pushed her down the stairs."

"Darla McFinkle?"

I nodded. "Haylee was stabbed, Jack. She didn't just fall down the stairs. Someone tried to kill the woman I love."

"Do you think Haylee was just out of it from hitting her head?"

"She sounded certain. She said Darla and then the word weapon. That was all she said."

Jack shook his head as we neared the hospital. "There was an incident at the parade today."

"What kind of incident? I know for a fact that Haylee was sleeping during the parade."

"An incident with Darla. They stripped her of her crown right before she was due to ride on the float as Strawberry Fest Princess. Rumor has it that Haylee gave the committee some damning piece of evidence to have her ousted."

My head shook instantly. "Haylee wouldn't do that. She doesn't start problems with that woman. She knows better."

"I'm going to hang around at the hospital and see if I can talk to Haylee myself. If I have to wait while they stabilize her, I'll have to call a committee member and ask them what happened today. If Darla did do this, and after what happened a few weeks ago, I wouldn't doubt she's capable of it, I'll have to pick her up and bring her in."

"Haylee has to be okay," I murmured, tuning out everything but how far away I was from the woman I loved. "She has to be okay. I just asked her to be my girlfriend, did you know that?" I asked him, my mind going a thousand miles a minute. "She's so beautiful and talented. I can't lose her now. I can't."

He pulled the car into the roundabout at the hospital ER and grasped my shoulder. "You're not going to lose her. She's going to come out of this and keep loving you for a million more cupcakes. Take a deep breath and square yourself before you go in there. She's going to need you to be calm and steady for her right now."

"Calm, right." I stared at my hands, red with her blood. "I need to wash my hands."

He climbed out of the car and opened my door, waiting for me to get out before we hit the doors of the ER running. "I'll find out where she is while you wash up in there," he said, pointing to the public restroom by the entrance. Meet me at the desk."

I did what he ordered, and while I scrubbed my hands, I forced my mind to stop thinking that if Darla did do this, I would kill her myself. I would have to let the law deal with her because no one was going to drag me away from the bed of the woman I love, now or ever again.

Twenty-Four

Good God, everything hurts. I tried to straighten myself in the bed, but it brought on a wave of pain and nausea that I wasn't expecting. A cold cloth was on my head, and a warm hand was on my arm, the two sensations warring with my muddled brain.

"You're okay, baby," Brady whispered, his other hand coming down on the wet cloth on my head. "Just take it slow and don't try to move too quickly."

"What happened?" I muttered with a mouth full of cotton.

"You don't remember?" he asked, his voice nonjudgmental and comforting.

I rocked my head on the pillow a couple of times and sorted through the gauzy haze in my brain, pushing aside the headache to sort through the last few hours of my life. My breath hitched, and I moaned. "Oh, God, it was Darla."

My eyes came open and stared directly into Brady's ice blue ones. Those eyes told me he was scared, and I instantly felt terrible for making him feel that way. My hand came up to cup his cheek, his beard prickly against my palm. "I'm sorry," I said, emotion clogging my throat. "I'm sorry. I should have been smarter."

He tenderly grasped my hand against his face. "Shh, it's over now. I'm going to take care of you. This wasn't your fault, cupcake. Let me call Officer Stevens in before you tell me what happened. He's been waiting for you to wake up so he could talk to you."

"I need a drink." My mouth was so dry and sticky that I was afraid I'd never swallow again.

He held the cup and straw for me while I drank thirstily, finally pulling it back from my lips. "Not too much at a time, or you'll get sick," he said with a smile. "Let me get Officer Stevens."

He jogged out of the room, and I tried to sort out what happened to make sure I told him everything in the right order. It wasn't going to be easy when my mind was so scattered, and my body hurt so badly. My shoulder was on fire, and my neck felt like someone hit it with a baseball bat. Add to that the pain in my heart when faced with Brady, knowing he was going to leave me sooner rather than later, and a tear ran down my face before I could stop it.

He returned at that moment, and his frantic gaze landed on mine, zeroing in on the tears immediately. "Hey, it's okay," he promised, wiping the tear with the cloth from my forehead. "God, I love you so much, cupcake. My heart has been on pause in my chest for the last three hours since I found you." His hand was in his hair, and I swallowed down the sob bubbling up in my throat.

More tears fell, and I wasn't able to say what I wanted to say, so I just bit my lip to keep it from trembling while he wiped the tears.

"Officer Stevens will be right in. Take a few deep breaths, sweetheart. I know you're out of sorts."

"Why does my shoulder feel like it's on fire?" I asked, trying to look at it, but my head hurt, and I got dizzy if I moved my eyes that way.

"You had a wound there that the doctors had to close in surgery. The doctor said it was to the fascia and tissue, but no other damage. He was able to close it up on the inside and then close the incision on the outside. He said you'd have a small scar, but he did the best he could to make it less noticeable."

"Surgery?" I asked, confused. "How did I end up with a wound on my shoulder?"

"The doctors said it was a stab wound," he said, his lips in a thin line.

"Haylee, man, it's good to see you awake," Jack said from the doorway as he walked into the room.

I waved and smiled the best I could. "Hi," I said weakly. "I didn't mean to hold you up."

"It's no problem, Haylee. I wanted to touch base with you because some of the things you told Brady before they brought you in were concerning."

I nodded, which I instantly regretted. My brain bounced around inside my skull, and I put my hand to my head to make it stop. "It was Darla," I managed to say. "She was waiting for me."

Brady had his hand on my hip, holding it tenderly to remind me he was there. I don't know why it mattered to me so much since I knew he was leaving, but it did. It mattered that he cared enough to keep soothing me when I struggled to make sense of this attack. I held onto that warm spot on my hip for all it was worth. "When you left the apartment?"

"Yes," I agreed, remembering not to nod. "I decided to start baking early, and it was just after midnight." I gasped and grabbed for Brady. My coordination was absent, and I missed his shirt by a mile. "The baking! There are so many special orders!"

"Shh," he said calmly. "Everything is taken care of at the bakery. I'll explain after you tell Jack what happened."

My heart was pounding out of my chest, and the monitors showed it, a warning beep filling the room until Brady started breathing with me to slow my heart rate again.

"Slow your breathing down, or they'll kick us out," he warned, watching the monitor until my heart rate went back to normal. "Good," he said, smiling encouragingly, "you've got this."

"You were going down to the bakery to start work," Jack said, and I nodded, scooting up higher in the bed, grateful when it didn't send shooting pain through me. "I was halfway down the steps when Darla stepped away from the building. She was slurring her words, and I immediately smelled the alcohol on her breath. She walked up the stairs and trapped me in, so I couldn't go up or down."

"And you fought?"

My head started to shake until I remembered not to do that. "No, she was angry that they took her crown away from her before she got on the float for the parade. Said she was tired of me playing the victim, and she was angry that I recorded her without her permission."

"When you recorded the incident at the cupcake bake-off?" Jack asked.

"Yeah. I explained that I didn't know the phone was still recording, but since it caught the exchange, I wanted the committee to know the kind of person they had representing the community. I stood up for myself for once against the woman and look at what happened."

Brady's hand came up to smooth the hair back off my forehead, his smile soft and loving. "I'm proud of you for having the courage to take that to the committee. You did the right thing, and you didn't deserve this."

Jack agreed with Brady. "He's right. You've put up with enough from her over the years, and you've always been gracious about it. The fact is, you could have done more with that footage than spoken privately to the committee about it. They could have done more than speak to her privately. They could have told everyone the truth instead of saying Darla decided she didn't have time to perform the duties of the crown and gave it to the runner-up."

My brow went down in concentration. "Is that what happened?"

"According to Mrs. Mulberry, when I spoke to her earlier, yes. It was done quietly, in private, and without public knowledge of the reasons why."

"Well, you know Darla. Once she feels slighted, it's all over."

Cupcake

"It's going to be all over," he agreed, pointing at my shoulder. "What happened after Darla spouted off?"

"I remember telling her not to step foot on my property again, and she got mad that I was always rubbing in how successful I was. Then she said she could make me unsuccessful. Next thing I know, I'm staring up at the stars from the bottom of the steps, and she's spitting on me."

"Spitting on you? Good God," Brady said, his face filled with fury. "You better find her first, Stevens."

"Don't threaten someone in front of a cop, Brady," I scolded.

Jack pointed at me. "What she said, but trust me, I will find her. What happened after you were pushed?"

I rubbed my forehead with frustration. "I don't remember. I think I passed out. She was reaching for something, and I remember thinking it was probably a gun, and I was going to die there. I just couldn't keep my eyes open or even move to get away from her."

I was shaking, and Brady was holding both of my hips now, trying to calm me. "It's okay. You're here, and you're safe. They're going to find her, and she will be held accountable for this."

Jack put his notebook away and nodded, a grim look on his face. "I can't believe I'm going to have to arrest Darla, but I am. You didn't stab yourself. I will let you know when we have her. There are officers searching the area around the bakery for the knife right now. I have another one sitting on her house. If she's home, they will take her into custody, and we'll book her."

I moaned and rocked my head back and forth. "No, please don't," I begged. "That will just cause more problems with her. I don't want that. I can't deal with it anymore. I'm too tired."

Brady had me in his arms now, as awkward as it was, and he tried to calm me with his lips to my temple. "Cupcake, they're going to charge her with a crime. You don't have to be afraid anymore."

"What?" I asked, wanting to sit up, but he held me down, refusing to let me go. "You can't do that. She didn't mean to hurt me. She was drunk!"

Jack shook his head. "I'm afraid the fact that she stabbed you says otherwise. I suspect the only reason you aren't dead is that Brady pulled up and spooked her. If he hadn't come in early tonight, this could have turned out a whole lot differently. The first thing that has to happen when you are up on your feet again is better lighting around the bakery. Motion sensor lights would have scared her away and given her no chance to take you by surprise. Do you understand me?"

I nodded mutely, refusing to look at Brady because he'd been telling me that for years.

"Good. I'll let you rest. Brady will be kept abreast of the situation with Darla, but we will need you to give a recorded statement at the station once you're able. In the meantime, rest up. The town needs their cupcakes."

I chuckled and nodded, tears in my eyes at his kindness. "Thank you, Jack. I appreciate your dedication here tonight."

"It's what we do. Just take care of yourself and leave the rest to us."

He waved as he walked out, and I let my head drop back to the pillow, tears on my face as I thought about the implications of what my life had become. "Trials, and cameras, and statements, and court," I moaned.

"What?" Brady asked, resting me back on the pillow and sitting by my side in the chair by the bed.

"That's what I'll have to face once they arrest her. Amber!" I exclaimed, frantic again at the thought of my best friend at the bakery alone. "Someone has to protect Amber!"

His hand grasped my chin to hold me in place. "Amber is fine, honey. She's at the bakery helping the officers. I've been keeping her updated about your condition, and she will be here as soon as she can."

"But the bakery," I said, another tear falling. I swiped it away angrily. "Why am I crying all the time?" I asked, frustrated.

"When you have a head injury, it is difficult to control your emotions. The doctors said it would improve over the next few days."

"That makes sense." I propped my hand on my forehead. "I have to get out of here. I have special orders to bake and a bakery to run. I can't let Darla ruin my business, especially now that you won't be working there anymore."

His gasp and the stricken look on his face wasn't what I was expecting. Before I could say anything more, a nurse strode into the room to take my vital signs. He stood and left my room, and likely, my life.

I had my hand buried in my hair and my heart in my throat. What did Haylee mean I wasn't going to be working there anymore? I grabbed my phone and punched in a number, waiting anxiously while it rang in my ear.

"Is she okay, Brady?" Amber asked without greeting me.

"Yeah, she's okay," I said without hesitation. "She's awake and talking. Sore, but she's going to be fine. She's asking about you, and I promised her you'd be over once you were done at the bakery."

"But she wants out of there so she can get the bakery open, right?" she asked on a chuckle.

"Exactly," I said slowly, and she noticed.

"What's wrong, Brady?"

I cleared my throat and leaned against the wall, willing my exhausted mind not to mess with my emotions any more tonight. "Haylee just said that she couldn't let Darla ruin her business now that I won't be working there anymore. Is she firing me, Amber? Just be honest with me, please," I begged. I didn't even care how lame or emasculated I sounded. I had to know what I did so I could fix it.

Amber was silent for a beat before she spoke. "I have no idea what you're talking about, Brady. She said nothing to me about you leaving. She's been weird since the bake-off, though. She was out at the van when I got there, and then suddenly, she just took off and said she didn't care what you thought about her leaving without you. I didn't get a chance to talk to her before everything went down. Maybe it's just the head injury or anesthesia talking? Is she confused?"

"Could be," I said, my heart loosening a little bit in my chest. "The nurse just left her room. I'm going to go talk to her and see if I can figure out what's going on."

"Okay, the police are wrapping everything up here, and then I'm going to wait for Taylor to arrive before I come over."

"There's no bread," I said immediately. "Please apologize to the customers."

"Don't worry. I'm sure word is out by now about what happened. We'll be here for the special orders, and the rest doesn't matter. Just take care of my girl."

"You got it," I said, nodding once. "After you get here, I'll head over to the bakery and get the product made for tomorrow. If I can't do anything else for her, I can at least keep the business running. That is if she doesn't fire me when I walk back in that room."

"She's not going to, and if she does, I'll kick her ass when I get there. She loves you, Brady. I don't know what's going on, but we'll get to the bottom of it. I'm half of this business, and I get a say in what goes on in it, too."

"Okay, thanks, Amber. See you soon."

I hung up the call and sucked in a breath to steel my nerves and get my head into focus before I walked back into her room. When I stopped in the doorway, she was sitting up higher in the bed and sipping water from the cup the nurse must have given her.

She startled when she saw me and coughed on the water. "I thought you left."

I shook my phone in my hand. "No, I was updating Amber. She's almost done with the police, and then she'll be over," I said, sitting down next to her in the chair again. "Once she gets here, I'm going to go back to The Fluffy Cupcake and get some product made for tomorrow. There aren't any special orders for cupcakes, but there are the buns and bread that the restaurants need."

"What about all the special orders for today?" she fretted, her hand on her forehead. "Amber will have to call them all."

"They're done," I promised her, wanting to touch her but afraid to at the same time. "I stayed late yesterday and finished them. I knew you weren't feeling well, and I wanted to get you ahead of the game for tonight's baking. Now I'm really glad I did."

"You did? Seriously?"

I nodded my agreement. "Just try to relax, Haylee. I've got your back just like I always do. Amber and I will keep the bakery running until you're feeling better."

"But—but you're leaving," she stuttered, her words tripping over her tongue. "You said you were leaving."

My hand strayed to her forehead against my will and brushed the hair back. "Did you dream that, cupcake? I never said I was going anywhere."

"I heard you!" she exclaimed, a tear falling down her face. Suddenly, her emotional issues made more sense. She honestly believed that a dream she had was real. "You told someone on the phone at the festival on Friday that your application had been approved and you had two job offers already. I think it was your old boss, and he wanted you to run his bakery."

My hand froze mid-stroke, and I tipped my head to the side. "Is that why you took off with the van and refused to answer the door?"

"I didn't need you to keep lying to my face about how much you loved me!" she exclaimed, knocking my arm away. "I heard you tell Mr. Cavanaugh that you can't date someone like me with no self-esteem!"

"Whoa, Haylee, no. I never said that."

"Don't lie to me, Brady! I heard you tell him that!"

I gently rubbed her hip since I knew she couldn't reach my hand to knock it away. "I think you overheard something with no context, and that messed with your head, Haylee. I did say that to Mr. Cavanaugh—"

"See, I'm not delusional!" she exclaimed.

"Shh, let me finish," I said patiently. I knew the head injury was making her volatile, but I wouldn't let her keep thinking I didn't want to be with her. "I did say those things, but we weren't talking about you."

"Who were you talking about then? You said you dated her for a couple of weeks, but you told me you hadn't dated anyone for a couple of weeks. I'm it. I'm the only one!"

"I stretched the truth on that one a bit. I didn't want him to think I was a total jackass for dropping Darla halfway through a date."

"What? Darla?"

I nodded, biting my lip to keep from smiling. "Mr. Cavanaugh was under the impression that I was dating Darla, so he was surprised to see the two of us so friendly during the competition. I guess he caught me giving you that kiss when we won."

"The whole town caught you," she said, a chuckle escaping, which was better than tears. "You weren't exactly subtle."

"You don't have to be when you're kissing your girlfriend, and you're in love. Make no mistake, I do love you, and you're still my girlfriend."

"I was so hurt," she whispered, her hand rubbing her chest absently. I covered it with mine and held them there together. "You had just asked me to be your girlfriend, and the next day you were telling people you couldn't be with me anymore."

My head swung wildly as I wiped away another tear that had escaped down her cheek. "No, sweetheart. That's not it at all. I want to be with you all the time. The last thirty-six hours have been so hard wondering why you wouldn't talk to me. Then I find you half-dead on the ground, and I knew I should have made you talk to me. If I hadn't given up so easily, I would have been there to protect you."

"You didn't know I told the committee about the confrontation. I should have predicted Darla would come after me, but I didn't even think about it. You were right all these years. I should have better lighting back there."

"I'll be calling someone to fix that situation as soon as I get back to the bakery," I agreed. "I'll never leave you open to an attack like that again, cupcake." I stroked her hair back, pain evident in my voice as I gazed at her.

"You won't be here to know," she said, her voice heavy with sadness. "You said your application was approved, so you'll be in Milwaukee running a bakery, which," she added, holding up her hand, "you deserve. You deserve to be the head of a bakery, and you won't get that at The Fluffy Cupcake."

"I wish you'd stuck around a few more minutes to have heard the rest of the conversation," I whispered. "My application was approved for master baker."

Her brow went down to her nose, and her breath hitched in her chest. "Wait, you passed?"

I nodded, a giant smile on my face. "That was the call I got before the judging. That was my big news. I passed, cupcake!" I couldn't help the excitement in my voice and how much I wanted to share it with her. "I've been dying to tell you, but I refused to do it over text."

"That's wonderful, Brady. Congratulations," she said, her chin wobbling with emotion. "You deserve this. You worked hard and were devoted to the process, and now it has paid off. I'm proud of you. Everything makes more sense now. That's why you can run a bakery."

"I can, but I won't be. You didn't hear the part where I told Baker Robinson that I couldn't run his bakery because my whole life was in Lake Pendle now. I found the woman I want to spend the rest of my life with, and I'm not leaving her for anything."

"You're staying?" she asked, her voice hopeful but desperate at the same time.

"I was never going anywhere to begin with, Haylee. You're my whole life now. I have every intention of working with you and loving you forever."

Tears were falling down her cheeks, and she reached her hand out for me to take. "My heart was shattered in so many pieces when I heard you say those things. I didn't know what to do, so I ran."

"Shh," I whispered, nose-to-nose with her now. "I wish you had just come and talked to me, baby. In the future, don't run, unless you're running to me. Promise me."

She nodded, her chin trembling with fear, anguish, relief, and fatigue. "I promise. I might need you to remind me for another thirty years or so, though."

"Only thirty?" I teased, kissing her lips carefully since she still had the oxygen tube in her nose. "I was thinking at least fifty or sixty." I stroked her cheek, her eyelids drooping the longer I did. "Sleep now. When you wake up, I might be at the bakery, but Amber will be here. Don't get scared because I didn't leave you. I'm just going to protect our business the same way I'll always protect you, with all my love and devotion."

Her lips pulled up in a smile as her eyes closed all the way, and finally, she slept.

Twenty-Five

I glanced down at the six-inch gash on my shoulder after I took the bandage off. There was no redness or signs of infection, so I finished cleaning it and covered it with the special bandage the hospital had sent home with me yesterday. At least I managed to get out of the hospital for my thirtieth birthday.

Last night was not exactly the party I was hoping for, and tonight wouldn't be either, but that was okay. I was just grateful to be alive. Being attacked by Darla had brought into focus what was important in this life. That red X on my calendar came to mind again, and I chuckled as I shut the light off in the bathroom and walked into the kitchen for my phone. I tapped the calendar, still missing the July page, and tisked my tongue. "You don't own me anymore."

It didn't own me. Brady Pearson owned me, and I was completely okay with it. We owned each other's hearts and never had I understood how much than over the last couple of days. His devotion to me at the hospital was palpable, and his dedication to my business when he only left my bedside to make sure it stayed running, told me he would always be my better half.

It was almost three in the afternoon, and Brady had been up to check on me several times during the day. He refused to let me go down to the bakery and do anything, so I had to cool my heels up here most of the day. That was okay. My head still bothered me if I did too much, so it was wiser to give it a few more days before I had to work around dangerous equipment again. After so much lazing around, I needed to stretch out my arm, so when Brady called to say he needed me in the bakery for some help with the ordering, I jumped at the chance. It gave me an excuse to check on everything without looking like a worrywart, too. I know Brady and Amber have everything in hand, but it would make it easier to relax if I got to check things out for myself.

I checked my phone, and there was another email from another committee member apologizing for the Darla fiasco, as people had taken to calling it. Truth be told, the fiasco was no one's fault but hers. I felt bad that others felt like they needed to apologize for her. She could do her own apologizing in court. The district attorney had to decide on charges, but from what I'd been told, she was going to be swimming in hot water for a long time to come.

Once the police took her into custody, after finding her passed out on the floor in her living room, they had to put her in the drunk tank overnight just to get her conscious enough to talk. The knife she stabbed me with was found in her bathtub, which was a very strange place to put a weapon you committed a crime with if you ask me, but that's Darla.

I suspected she was going to claim a psychotic break or try to blame this on me, but for now, I was safe from her while she remained in jail until bail was set. After that, she wouldn't be allowed near me, or she'd risk going straight to jail without passing go. Did I doubt she'd try? No, but for her sake, I hoped she kept her distance. Not just because the law wouldn't be lenient, but because Brady wouldn't be.

I heard his footfalls on the stairs, and I opened the door, smiling when he stood at the top, his hair freshly washed and styled. He was dressed to the nines in khaki shorts and a button-down shirt.

"Well, hello, birthday girl," he said, kissing my lips lightly. "You look gorgeous. You're like a birthday cupcake that's good enough to eat."

"You've said that every time you've checked on me today."

"And I meant it every time," he agreed, a smile on his face.

I tugged at the front of his shirt gently. "You're a little dressed up to do bakery work," I said, confused.

"True, but the bakery work won't take long, and then I was hoping to celebrate your birthday. As long as you're feeling up to it, of course."

"I would love to," I assured him, pulling the door closed behind us. "I need to stretch out and move around a little. My arm doesn't bother me much now, and the incision looked good when I changed the bandage. I'll just have to be careful of my head. I wish I were able to make your anniversary cupcakes."

"It's okay," he assured me, kissing my lips. "We'll celebrate my anniversary when you're feeling up to it. Today, we're celebrating everything that's you. Take my arm when we go down, so you don't fall," he ordered.

I did as he instructed, letting him help me down the stairs. I would protest, but I knew it would do no good. Besides, he was probably right. Sometimes I still felt dizzy from the concussion, and it wasn't worth falling again just to be stubborn. Besides, I liked that he wanted to protect me. It made him feel better and gave him a way to put right in his head what happened.

"I owe you my life, Brady," I blurted out. "I don't know if I ever said thank you for finding me."

We stepped onto the ground at the bottom of the stairs, and he paused. "Cupcake, you don't have to thank me for finding you. I love you, and that's what you do when you love someone, remember?"

"Right now, when I think something, sometimes it comes out of my mouth before I can stop it," I explained with embarrassment.

"I know, and I also know I can't tell you not to think about it because your mind isn't quite right yet. Once it is, though, I don't want it to cross your mind again." He grasped my face and held me to his nose. "I love you so much. I'm beyond thankful we're here to celebrate this day together."

"I love you, too," I promised, kissing his lips to relax him. "You're really keyed up. I'm sorry for mentioning it."

He smiled and winked, his shoulders relaxing a little bit. "It's not your fault. I get that way when I think about losing you. I relive those seconds when I found you on the ground and my heart pounds to think about what would have happened if I hadn't come in early to talk to you. It will always scare me, and I've decided that's a good thing. The memory will always be there as a reminder that things can't go unsaid when you love someone." He shook out his shoulders and cleared his throat. "Okay, let's forget about it and go say hello to your bestie before we celebrate the big three-oh."

He opened the side bakery door, and I stepped in, the warmth of the space wrapping me in a hug like it always did. I inhaled deeply and sighed. "God, I love this place." I heard his chuckle behind me, and I knew he understood. "Did you get everything put together for tomorrow's orders?" I reached for the cooler handle and walked in to inspect everything. Brady stood behind me and pointed out all the cupcake orders and birthday cakes he'd decorated today.

I turned into his chest. "They're beautiful. You don't even need me around here anymore."

"Don't even think about leaving me with all these cakes," he teased, tweaking my nose. "I don't like decorating. That's your strength."

"And these beautiful white and rye bread braids are yours. They're gorgeous."

"So are you," he said, backing me up against a rack and planting a kiss on me that was reminiscent of the first one we shared here a month ago. This time, it was a little bit more reserved, and he was content to be gentle while still filling me with passion and desire.

"I know I promised not to do that here ever again, but I didn't think you'd mind."

"Not at all, Able Baker Brady," I promised. "As your boss, I'm going to make you take that promise back today. I think if you have a choice between kissing in the cooler and not kissing in the cooler—"

His lips stopped the words coming from my mouth, and I moaned softly in my throat, the sensation reminding me that I hadn't died out there. I made it to my thirtieth birthday to stand here and be kissed silly by a man who loved me as much as I loved him. Maybe even more, if that was possible. He sure was trying to prove it was.

"Always kiss in the cooler," he said, lifting his lips off mine. "We better go say hello to Amber before she catches us necking in the cooler."

"Again," I added, following him out and closing the door behind me.

Brady took my hand and held it behind his back as we walked into the main bakery. I braced myself, expecting a few of our regulars to be there still. They'd want to make sure I was okay before they left. I had stayed reclusive since I arrived home yesterday for that reason. I had no less than thirty people visit me in the hospital before the nurse finally stopped allowing visitors so I could get some rest. When I stepped around Brady to look for Amber, I froze in my tracks.

The whole place was jam-packed with people who all stood up and whispered, "Surprise!" with their hands waving in the air.

"I told them they would have to be quiet because of your head," Brady explained, a smirk on his face.

I noticed the banner that said, "Happy 30th birthday, Cupcake!" and started laughing as tears filled my eyes. "Thank you, everyone!" I exclaimed, genuine excitement flowing through me to see all the people who have supported me over the years come together to wish me a happy birthday.

Brady led me to a table where Amber stood holding a birthday sash. I hugged her fiercely, her laughter filling my head and adding joy to the day. "Hello, birthday girl. I'm surprised we managed to pull this off without you catching on," she said, helping me sit and then sliding the sash over my head. "We couldn't let this day go unrecognized in the face of everything you've been through this year. I'm so proud of you for everything you've overcome and for your strength in the face of what happened. You're my hero," she whispered, hugging me carefully.

It was then that everyone gathered around to laugh with me quietly, encourage me softly, and remind me that in this place, everyone was family.

"How are you holding up?" Brady asked, joining me at the table while everyone snacked on cake and coffee.

"I'm good," I promised him. "This was so sweet of you." I hugged him tightly around his neck. "I didn't see it coming."

"The fact that you were in the hospital for a couple of days helped with that," he said on a chuckle, patting my back. "Did I pass the birthday cake test?"

I leaned back and eyed the giant sheet cake. "I had one piece, but I can't decide if it was good or not. I might need another one to make a final decision."

Brady tickled my side gently, and I laughed, being careful not to pull anything when I scrambled away from him in my seat. "I know Orange Creamsicle is your favorite cake."

"It totally is, and it was delightfully delicious. I didn't appreciate the message, though." I dropped my brow to look fierce, but the smile on my face probably gave me away. "Lordy, lordy, Cupcake's thirty? It doesn't even rhyme."

He snorted to hold back the laughter and gave me the palms up. "It was Amber's idea, I swear."

"Oh, sure, blame the best friend," I said on a wink. "I'll be taking it out of your hide later tonight. Hope you're prepared."

"I literally could not be more prepared, but I think we should probably hold that thought for a few more days until you don't have stitches in your shoulder and a head injury."

"We can be resourceful," I said mysteriously.

Brady stood and motioned for everyone to listen. "I just wanted to say thank you to everyone who helped me pull off this little party today and to thank you all for coming. It was almost a week ago when Haylee told me that someone else's assessment of her wasn't wrong. She was an orphan, and she could count the number of friends she had on one hand. I'm so glad you all proved her wrong today. I also know that this is only a small sampling of the people in this town who care about Haylee. The fire marshal was adamant about that capacity limit," he said, shaking his head. "Kidding, but the truth is, if she hadn't been injured, I'd planned to hold this party at the beach where the whole town could come to wish her a happy day."

"And you could do some fancy footwork out on the water!" Mrs. Mulberry called out.

Brady pointed at her and chuckled. "I might have, she's a real sucker for me in that wetsuit."

It was my turn to laugh, and I rolled my eyes at the same time because I was, even if I was going to pretend for the rest of my life that I wasn't.

"Since her injuries didn't allow for that kind of party today, I decided I'd have to hold a small one today and that bigger one a little later on when she was feeling up to it."

"Brady," I hissed, "the party has been wonderful. I wasn't even expecting a party."

"I know you weren't, cupcake," he said, getting down on one knee. "I bet you aren't expecting this either, but I'm

203

still going to do it." He reached into his pocket and pulled out a black box, cracking open the lid to reveal a sparkling diamond solitaire that made my breath catch in my chest. "Haylee, since the day I walked into The Fluffy Cupcake, I've been smitten by your beauty, your ever-present gigantic smile, and the magic you find in the confections you bake here. I learned over the years that people don't come to The Fluffy Cupcake just to get cupcakes. They come to get joy. They come here because at the best of times and the worst of times in their lives, you are always here for them. You provide memories that bring them together, even when life may have separated them. You do the same thing for me. Every memory I have from the last seven years somehow involves you. The ways you picked apart my sourdough until I refused to make anything else until I got it right," he said, shaking his head. I wanted to laugh, but I was too frozen in place by the ring and the man on bended knee before me. His words were echoing through my head and my heart like a drumbeat of peace.

"Brady, we've only been dating for a month," I whispered.

The crowd chuckled, and so did Brady. "You're right, but ask anyone here today if me on one knee, holding out a ring to you, surprises any of them. Go ahead. I'll wait."

I glanced up and around the room. Everyone was shaking their heads back and forth without hesitation. Amber was crying as she recorded the whole thing, and Mrs. Mulberry was clapping quietly by her chin, her eyes filled with tears and a smile on her face. Amber's mom and dad were grinning like Cheshire cats and holding hands like they were still newlyweds.

"Maybe we've only officially been dating a month, but all of those everyday little things that we do together here have built the foundation of our love story. I love you, and I don't want to wait any longer to officially call you *my* cupcake. Haylee Davis, will you do me the honor of becoming my wife?"

My chin was trembling when I lifted my head from the ring to gaze into his eyes. They were so full of love, honor, and a speck of fear that my tears spilled over my lashes. "You want me to marry you?" I stuttered, my brain having paused when he cracked the box open. "Are you sure?"

He chuckled and grasped my hand, holding it tightly in his. "As sure as I was the day I accepted the position as kitchen manager at a little bakery in a town no one had ever heard of before. I knew then that I was going to marry you. I've waited seven years to ask this question, but if you need more time, I will wait for seven more."

I shook my head slowly, and his eyes dimmed a bit with frustration. "No, I don't need more time. I love you, Brady. I don't want to wait seven more years to marry you. I don't even want to wait seven more days."

"Is that a yes?" Mrs. Mulberry asked in a stage whisper.

I chuckled and winked at him, the relief on his face filling my heart with so much love it nearly burst. "Yes, I'll marry you, Brady Pearson."

He had the ring on my finger before I blinked, and then he picked me up in a hug, swinging me back and forth gently, his lips to my ear. "I love you, cupcake."

"And I love you. As it turns out, you can have your cake and eat it, too," I promised, the light of forever filling his eyes when his lips talked mine into being his today, tomorrow, and always.

Tart

The Fluffy Cupcake Book 2
Coming Soon!

My name is Amber Phyllis Larson, and I'm terrified of thunderstorms. Embarrassing for a woman of thirty to admit, but there it is in a nutshell. At three a.m. on a Wednesday morning in late May, it was dark, the skies were heavy with rain, and thunder rumbled in the distance over Lake Pendle. We shouldn't have to deal with thunderstorms this early in the season in Minnesota, but someone forgot to tell Mother Nature that.

I popped a pod of coffee into the machine and waited while it spit the rich, black coffee into my travel mug. Whoever said the early bird gets the worm had never worked in a bakery for nine years. I didn't just work in a bakery for nine years, though. I'd been the co-owner of The Fluffy Cupcake with my best friend, Haylee, for all nine of those bliss-filled years. She was recently married to Brady Pearson, her partner in crime at the baker's bench and now in life. That left me, the only one of the dynamic duo to remain single, much to my mother's chagrin. Unlike Haylee or my mother, I didn't see being single at thirty as the end of the world.

I chuckled to myself when I snapped the lid on my travel mug and turned off the kitchen light. Last year, Haylee decided she had to be in a committed relationship before she turned thirty. She made that resolution on New Year's Eve, which only gave her seven months and thirteen days to find Mr. Wonderful. She was so focused on her goal that she was too obtuse to see that the perfect guy was already right in front of her face. So, I set her up with every guy I knew she wouldn't be able to tolerate for more than an hour, much less forever. I'm happy to report my plan worked. If she ever found out I tortured her on purpose, she wouldn't be amused, but sometimes, we need a little help to see what is directly in front of our face.

I grabbed my purse and slung it over my shoulder, taking a deep breath before I opened the door to my apartment. With any luck, I'd make it to the bakery before it started to storm any harder. I hated driving in lightning and thunder. Childish, I know, but if you'd lived my life the last seventeen years, you'd understand. I stuffed my thin athletic frame inside the car and slammed the door. Haylee was always jealous of the fact that I could eat anything I wanted from the bakery case without gaining a pound. I was always jealous of the fact that she had curves. What she saw as a negative feature, I would kill to have. Women are funny that way, I guess.

I shut off the engine in front of the bakery as the first drop of rain hit the windshield of my Subaru. I grabbed my purse and mug, limped to the door, and made it under the awning as the skies opened up and the rain sluiced down. When I unlocked the door and stepped inside, the smell of fresh bread and cakes hit me straight in the face. The scent was always like coming home. I loved that I worked in a place that brought so many people joy day after day, but I loved the people I worked with even more.

"Hey, Amber!" Brady yelled from the back of the bakery. "Glad you beat the rain in."

"Barely," I said as the first bolt of lightning lit up the sky. I darted away from the window and to the back of the bakery where I couldn't see it. I never said I wasn't a chicken. "Where's Hay-Hay?" I asked, grabbing my apron off the hook after I put my purse in the office.

"In the cooler. We have cupcakes coming out of our ears and no place to put them."

I pointed at him. "That's why I came in early. I figured you guys were going to be scrambling to get the order ready for the school this morning."

Brady laughed and went back to his bread kneading. "Scrambling is an understatement. I'm sure she would appreciate the help. I have to finish the standing bread and bun orders."

Brady had become a master baker last summer and was now in charge of all the bread baking for The Fluffy Cupcake. Haylee was in charge of the pastries, cakes, and cupcakes, which meant with an order the size she had today, she was going to need help, or our bakery case would be empty this morning.

A clap of thunder boomed overhead, and I darted for the cooler, glad Brady had his back to me. Did I mention that I hate storms? I grabbed a jacket off the hook and slipped it on, then opened the cooler door and stepped in. I wasn't upset to be in the cooler. It was our safe place for severe weather, and you couldn't see the lightning inside.

"Hey, cupcake," I said, gazing at the scene before me. "It looks like a cupcake apocalypse in here."

Haylee stood up and blew out a breath, the action rustling the hair that had fallen over her forehead. "Why did I think this was a good idea?"

"I don't know what the problem is, Hay-Hay. I mean, forty-one dozen cupcakes are like no big deal," I said, flipping my hand around while I imitated her. "That's what you told me when I asked if I should take the order again this year."

She rolled her eyes and went back to her cupcake counting. "It's not a big deal when I thought I was going to make generic cupcakes. When I found out they wanted the school logo on each one, then it became a big deal."

I peeked at the tray of cupcakes closest to me and grinned. "They look great, though! Look at the cute penguins." The Lake Pendle Penguins was the school's logo, and even growing up here, I never entirely understood it. We don't have penguins in Minnesota.

"They're cute, but they're a pain in my gigantic ass," she muttered, putting together another cake box to start packing cupcakes. At this rate, it will only take nine hundred boxes to transport them all to the school. Maybe that was dramatic. It will only take thirteen. I started putting together another box and helped her move all of the cupcakes from pans to boxes.

"I know the kids at the elementary school are going to love them, Hay-Hay. They're cute, and we all know they're going to be delicious." Another boom of thunder shook the cooler, and I leaned back against the shelf, covering my ears and waiting for it to pass before I started packing again. I didn't want to drop a cupcake and get in trouble with the baker.

Haylee came over and rubbed my back a couple of times. "You're okay. The weatherman said it's just passing showers and storms today. Nothing severe."

I nodded and let out the breath I'd been holding. "You know I'm a chickenshit, but I'll be fine."

She started on the next box of cupcakes. "You're not a chickenshit. You went through a lot, and you're entitled to carry scars because of it."

We packed the next four boxes of cupcakes in silence, my fingers able to count the forty-eight cupcakes for each box without even having to think about it. When most of them were packed, I glanced around the almost empty cooler.

"There's not much product here for the case," I observed.

Haylee pointed out the door of the cooler. "Able Baker Brady is baking off all the cupcakes and cakes we need for today. They should be cooling on the racks by now. I'll decorate everything when I finish here. I kept it simple for today since we had all of these cupcakes going out the door. It's a Tuesday, so three flavors of cupcakes will be enough."

"I should have known you had it under control," I said on a head shake. "You've never not had it under control."

She frowned, and her eyes clouded for a moment. "Well, there was that one time."

My arms went around her for a gentle hug. "And that one time wasn't your fault."

It was just a few days before Haylee's birthday last July when Darla McFinkle attacked her. She thought Haylee had cost her the title of Strawberry Fest Princess, but at nearly thirty, Darla shouldn't have been running for the crown. Darla always did what Darla wanted to do, though. She'd bullied Haylee her entire life, and it culminated with Darla trying to kill my best friend behind our bakery. If Brady hadn't found her when he did, Darla might have succeeded. I was so glad she was still here with me every day.

"Have you heard anything about the trial?" I asked, sliding the last box onto the rack we'd push out to the delivery van later.

She grimaced, and her eyes went to the ceiling. "Jury selection starts next week. She's hired the best attorney in the state, so she'll probably walk."

"Where does she get the money to pay for that?" I asked stymied. "She hasn't worked a day in her pathetic thirty years of life."

"Daddy," Haylee said, her eyes rolling. "Daddy has always spoiled her. He's the reason she's the way she is now."

"A murderer," I muttered, shaking my head.

"Innocent until proven guilty, Amber," she reminded me, and we both broke down into a fit of giggles.

"Hard to pretend you're innocent when you leave the knife you stabbed someone with in your bathtub, and your DNA all over their body."

"I'm sure she will find a way to twist it in her favor. She always does. Anyway, I think we're done here." She pointed at the cupcakes, but I knew she was talking about the discussion regarding Darla. She didn't like to talk about it, not that I could blame her, so I nodded my head in agreement.

"We're ready. Once Taylor comes in, I'll have Brady help me load these, and I'll deliver them. That way, you can finish your work."

She slung her arm over my shoulders and squeezed me. "Thanks, bestie. I appreciate it. You're better at schmoozing with people than I am anyway."

"That's what makes us a great team," I said, throwing her a wink and heading to the front of the bakery to start the day.

The Lake Pendle School District consisted of three schools in different areas of the town. Lake Pendle Elementary sat near the lake in a sprawling brick building that had been around for only a few decades. Built new in the nineties to replace an old building past its prime, and fire codes, the new building was a source of pride for the community. With windows in all the classrooms, interior computer labs, and a beautiful gymnasium, the Lake Pendle Littles, as they're referred to, get a state-of-the-art education. I don't have kids, but I do know technology is more important than anything now that our world runs on it.

Today's event was for the Lake Pendle Littles and their Bigs. The elementary and high school partner together in a program to offer mentoring, support, friendship, and encouragement between schools. A high school freshman is paired with a first-grader, and they spend the next four years together, culminating in a graduation ceremony at the elementary for the fourth graders going to the middle school and the high schoolers moving on to college or transitioning to work life. It was a favorite event of the community, and in a few more hours, this place was going to be packed. Luckily for me, at just a little past seven, it was quiet, other than staff preparing for the day. Thankfully, the storms had petered out and left us with just a few rain showers on this Friday morning. Delivering thirteen giant boxes of cupcakes was easier when it wasn't raining, for obvious reasons.

I slammed the doors shut on the van and pushed the cart toward the side door of the elementary school, where deliveries were made to Cook Cramer. I swear Mrs. Cramer was timeless. She'd been cooking here since I was a kid, and since I'm thirty, that's a lot of years. In truth, I went to school with her kids, so she's not that old, but she is one of the most beloved figures in this school for both her fantastic food and her sweet nature. She didn't have time to make forty dozen cupcakes, though.

"Oaf," I said, nearly coming to a complete halt and grabbing boxes of cupcakes as they started to slide off the cart. "What the hell?" I exclaimed, standing with the last box before it hit the ground.

I stared into a face that was as surprised as mine was. "Sorry," the guy said, taking the box from my shaking hands and sliding it back onto the cart. "I had my back turned and didn't know you were coming."

"You couldn't hear the cart with the one rattling wheel coming up behind you?" I asked hotly. "I don't think the kids are going to appreciate smashed cupcakes for graduation. You were probably on your phone."

He held it up sheepishly, and I huffed. "I was, but in my defense, I was arguing with a teenager." Before I could answer, he stuck his hand out. "Bishop Halla."

I reluctantly shook his hand but didn't smile. "Amber Larsen. Halla. That's?"

"Finnish," he answered, hitting the doorbell by the kitchen door so Mrs. Cramer knew someone was waiting.

"I should have known since we are in Minnesota," I said, chuckling. Another crack of thunder filled the air, and I jumped, sliding under the awning over the door while silently begging Cook Cramer to hurry up.

Cupcake

"That's a long way away," he said nonchalantly.

"I know. Are you here for a reason?" I asked, wondering why he was hanging around.

He pointed at the door. "I'm a teacher. I'll go in this way, too."

"If you're a teacher here, don't you have a key?"

The door opened, and Mrs. Cramer peeked her head out. "Oh, Amber!"

"Hi, Mrs. Cramer. The Fluffy Cupcake has arrived with your, well, fluffy cupcakes."

She clapped excitedly and propped the door open. "You know it's graduation day when the cupcakes show up! Hey, good morning, Mr. Halla," she said, acknowledging the man standing next to me as she peered into a box. Her grin grew when she spotted all the penguins in their cuteness. "Adorable as always. Haylee is a cupcake goddess."

"You know it! I have thirteen of these boxes."

"I already made space. I'll unload this cart while you get the next load. There's another cart over there," she said, pointing to a metal cart by the wall. "You have about twenty minutes before the buses arrive and the kids start streaming in."

"I better move then," I said, heading to the door. "I don't want to be accosted by three-foot-tall cupcake thieves."

The man who I had forgotten was still standing there laughed heartily. "You've got them pegged. How about if I help you with the other boxes, and we'll make quick work of it?"

"Oh, you don't have to do that," I said instantly, grabbing the cart after swapping mine out with Mrs. Cramer. "You have work to do, I'm sure."

He set his bag and coffee mug down just inside the door of the kitchen and shrugged. "I can't do much until the kids arrive. Maybe if I help you bring the rest in, I'll feel less guilty about almost ruining the cupcakes."

I eyed him up and down then. He was ridiculously handsome standing there in his button-up dress shirt and

213

tie. The pink pinstriped shirt was tucked into his dress slacks, and his feet were adorned in a pair of Hush Puppies. The look was trendy and hip, but that wasn't what sucked me in. His face did that all by itself. His eyes were a luscious garnet green that drew you in and held you in his atmosphere whenever he spoke. Dammit. I was a sucker for green eyes. I could feel my resolve weakening about letting him help. He wore a beard tightly clipped to his skin, his hair slicked back and blended in to meet the beard, and a pair of lips that could kiss the heck out of you without breaking a sweat. Where the heck did that come from, Amber?

I realized I was staring at him, so I shrugged nonchalantly—so as not to look like I cared what he did—and started pushing the cart toward the van. "Suit yourself," I said as he walked beside me.

"I haven't seen you around before, Amber," he said, making conversation as we loaded the cart up with boxes.

"Then you must be new here. I've lived in Lake Pendle my entire life, and I run the bakery on Main Street. You don't have to look hard to find me."

He rose to his full height of over six feet, and I whimpered a little at how he was good enough to eat. I loved a tall, handsome man with a pair of eyes to get lost in. He was all of that and then some, which meant he had to be taken. Also, I'd sworn off men after the last debacle I'd dealt with over the winter.

He brushed off his hands and smiled. If possible, his smile made him even more handsome, and his straight white teeth weren't creepy when they peeked out from between his lips. Cripes. I desperately needed to get laid. I was ogling this guy like he was a fine cut of meat from Butcher Don's shop.

"I'm new here and haven't had time to investigate the bakery. You're always closed when I'm done with work, and I've been so busy setting up house on the weekends I keep forgetting to take a break."

"I see," I said, just as a bolt of lightning lit up the sky and the thunder followed almost instantly. I screamed and jumped into the back of the van, huddled there until the last of the thunder rumbled overhead.

"Hey, Amber, it's okay," he said softly.

I glanced up to see him kneeling on the floor of the van with one knee, his hands out to me to keep me calm. "Just a spring storm. It's not going to hurt you, but if we don't get these boxes inside, the rain is going to ruin them."

I was shaking, and my heart was pounding when I lowered my arms from over my head. I had to swallow around the lump in my throat before I could speak. "Sor—sorry. I overreacted. It took me by surprise." I stiffened my shoulders and climbed out of the van, slamming the doors closed again and grabbing the handle of the cart. He was carrying the sheet cake while I pushed the cart, and we hurried toward the entrance of the school to get inside before the rain started in earnest. We dodged inside just as the skies opened and the rain poured down again.

"Wow, just made it," he said, lowering the giant cake box to the counter before he grabbed his bag.

"Thanks for helping," I said, closing the door against the rain. I would have to wait out the storm before I headed back to the bakery.

"Anytime," he said, offering a wave before he disappeared through the door of the cafeteria.

That left me standing there staring after him, wishing I knew a whole hell of a lot more about Bishop Halla, but knowing that was never going to happen.

Girls like me don't end up with guys like him.

About the Author

Katie Mettner writes small-town romantic tales filled with epic love stories and happily-ever-afters. She proudly wears the title of *'the only person to lose her leg after falling down the bunny hill'* and loves decorating her prosthetic with the latest fashion trends. She lives in Northern Wisconsin with her own happily-ever-after and three mini-mes. Katie has a massive addiction to coffee and Twitter, and a lessening aversion to Pinterest — now that she's quit trying to make the things she pins.

You can find Katie on her website at www.Katiemettner.com

Other Books by Katie Mettner

The Kontakt Series (2)

The Sugar Series (5)

The Northern Lights Series (4)

The Snowberry Series (7)

The Kupid's Cove Series (4)

The Magnificent Series (2)

The Bells Pass Series (3)

The Dalton Sibling Series (3)

The Raven Ranch Series (2)

Someone in the Water (Paranormal)

White Sheets & Rosy Cheeks (Paranormal)

The Secrets Between Us

After Summer Ends (Lesbian Romance)

Finding Susan (Lesbian Romance)

Torched

Find all of Katie's Books on Amazon!

Printed in Great Britain
by Amazon

31161772R00126